Don't Tell, Don't Tell, Don't Tell

DON'T TELL, DON'T TELL, DON'T TELL

LIANE SHAW

Second Story Press

Library and Archives Canada Cataloguing in Publication

Shaw, Liane, 1959-, author
Don't tell, don't tell, don't tell / Liane Shaw.

Issued in print and electronic formats.
ISBN 978-1-927583-95-1 (paperback).
—ISBN 978-1-927583-99-9 (epub)

I. Title.

PS8637.H838D66 2016   jC813'.6   C2015-908404-0

C2015-908405-9

Edited by Carolyn Jackson and Kathryn Cole
Designed by Melissa Kaita
Cover illustration © iStockphoto

Printed and bound in Canada

*Second Story Press gratefully acknowledges the support of the
Ontario Arts Council and the Canada Council for the Arts for our
publishing program. We acknowledge the financial support of the
Government of Canada through the Canada Book Fund.*

ONTARIO ARTS COUNCIL
CONSEIL DES ARTS DE L'ONTARIO
an Ontario government agency
un organisme du gouvernement de l'Ontario

 Canada Council   Conseil des Arts
for the Arts   du Canada

Funded by the Government of Canada
Financé par le gouvernement du Canada

 Canadä

Published by
SECOND STORY PRESS
20 Maud Street, Suite 401
Toronto, ON M5V 2M5
www.secondstorypress.ca

For my precious nephew Braydon, who sees the world in colors that the rest of us can only dream about, and for his mother, Pam, who loves him for who he is without trying to change him into something more socially acceptable but infinitely less interesting.

It's so dark.

So much can be hiding in the blackness.

I have to move or something could happen to me.

Something else could happen to me.

I'm standing in a field with puke on my shoes and snot in my hair.

My life is completely over.

I can't tell anyone about this.

Ever.

I hate this place.

I just want to go home.

one

"Okay, Freddy. This won't take long. Just a few questions, and you can go. All right?"

He's staring directly at my eyes, so I know he's talking to me, but I don't have to answer him when he doesn't use my real name. It's a rule.

My rule.

I can see all sorts of people coming in and going out. I wonder how many people come here every day? Lots I bet. Hundreds of bodies spitting out thousands of words—millions of germs looking for someone to land on.

My skin is crawling so much I think it's leaving without me.

I want to go home.

"Fred! Can you look at me? I need you to pay attention."

My name isn't Fred, either. Or the Fredster. Or Ferd the

nerd. Or all of the other grosser names people like to call me that aren't my own.

"Frederick, honey. The officer is speaking to you. You need to pay attention."

Pay attention. Pay attention.

It feels like I'm in math class.

"All right. Pay attention everyone. I would like you to use the formula and calculate the value of C. Quickly, in your notebooks."

I pick up my pencil to do what I'm told. Number two. The best kind. Generic and mid-grade. Not too dark and not too light. Just right for things like tests. I like to be ready for tests. Tests are important. You get graded on them and that lets people know how smart you are, even if you already know how smart you are inside of your own mind. You aren't really supposed to keep your intelligence a secret. It doesn't really belong to you. Your teachers and parents think it belongs to them.

Some number two pencils are called HB pencils. It depends on where you buy them. HB means hard black.

I know lots about pencils because I googled it. I google most things that are important to me because googling fills me up with information that turns into thoughts and makes things interesting inside of my head.

"Frederick! The teacher is calling on you. Wake up!" I feel a sharp pain in my side as Robert pokes me with his pencil. Ow! Now I know why they're called *hard* black. Robert is a year older than me, but I'm in his math class because I have advanced skills. Robert is good at math also, but I'm better.

He's better at listening to the teacher, though. I look up. She's standing right beside my desk, glaring at me.

"Fred! You need to focus. You're daydreaming again."

"Frederick. Thirty-seven." The teacher looks at me as if she thinks my intelligence is hiding from her.

"Pardon?" Her intelligence seems to be hiding too.

"My name is Frederick, and twelve squared plus thirty-five squared is thirty-seven squared." I think I hear Robert laugh behind me, but I'm not sure.

"Oh, right. Good work, Fred. I guess you were paying attention after all."

Guess I'm the only one who paid it today.

"Frederick! Please focus. You need to talk to the officer!"

The loud voice startles me right out of math class, and I look up at my mother's face. She isn't looking at me, though. She's looking at a man. Not just a man. A police officer.

I'm at the police station because my mother said that the police wanted to speak with me. That's what she said when she came into my room this morning without knocking, which was a direct infringement on our room privacy agreement.

"Frederick! You have to get dressed and come with me now. The police want to talk to you!" Her voice shrieks through my door, high and shrill like a chipmunk yelling at you to stay away from his tree. The thought makes me smile a little, and she sees it because she comes in without an invitation.

"Why are you smiling? This isn't funny. The police called here and want me to take you down to the station. What is this about? What could they want with you?" She's not looking at me when she asks the questions, so I don't answer. She's always told me that you have to look directly at someone you want to have a conversation with.

Her rule.

"Answer me, Frederick. What do the police want with you? Did you see something or do something?"

I still don't answer because I'm not sure what she's asking. I see and do lots of somethings every day. She's leaving words out of her sentences because she's upset for some reason, and now she doesn't make sense.

"Frederick! Are you listening to me? We have to go and see the police!"

It's interesting the way people say "the police" as if you are going to see all of them. Or as if there is only one of them.

"Frederick. Pay attention to me. Please."

Pay attention. Pay attention.

I look at her eyes. I can't look anywhere else because she has my chin trapped in her fingers, and she's staring at me. She looks for answers inside my eyes, but she can't ever find them. Even though she wants me to keep my intelligence outside for everyone to see and judge, there's lots of pieces of me buried in here that she'll never ever find, even when she decides I'm a ketchup bottle that she can squeeze, so all of my answers come squirting out, red and dripping and making a messed-up conversation all over the floor. I don't like messes so I keep my true answers inside where it's clean.

"Just get dressed and come downstairs. We'll talk in the car." She leaves the room. Privacy for dressing. At least she remembered that.

I push back my blankets and slowly swing my legs over the side of the bed, looking down to make sure my slippers are precisely in their spots. I need slippers on before I touch the floor. My feet aren't impressed with the way my floor feels without slippers. I found that out a long time ago. I slip my slippers on, which makes the word sensible. Otherwise, *slippers* is just a silly word. Why would you want to wear something that was designed to make you slip? I wiggle my toes a bit to be sure they feel right.

Turn back to the bed and tuck all the sheets and blankets under the mattress. Nice and smooth, so you could bounce a nickel off them like in movies about the army. Not sure why it's important to be able to bounce a nickel off your bed, but I tried it once and it worked. If it's still smooth and nickel-friendly at bedtime, I'll be able to get back in.

Unbutton my top next, starting from the bottom. I used to count the buttons when I was little just to practise. Sometimes I still do it accidentally, as if I forgot that I grew up. One, two, three, four, five. Five is a good number. I like prime numbers best.

I only wear shirts with buttons. I don't like shirts that can trap you. It happened to me once when I was smaller than I am now. It was a strange shirt, too tall at the neck. Mother put it over my face and tried to pull on it. The too tall part blinded my eyes and got stuck in my mouth so I couldn't breathe. Because I couldn't breathe, I couldn't scream for help, so I just let myself fall to the floor. That way I could feel dead before the shirt actually killed me. Playing dead is a good way to make grizzly bears leave you alone, but you should never try it with black bears because it might result in you getting eaten, even though black bears are much smaller than grizzly bears. But playing dead worked with my mother because it made her notice me. At least for a while it did, when I was little.

My mother's closer to black-bear size, although she would be angry if I said that out loud because she says that women don't like to have their size talked about for some strange reason that I don't understand.

When I was really small, I had a wooden toy box that my poppa made for me. When I needed to go away for a while, I would take out all of my toys and climb into my coffin, so I could be dead.

My mother didn't like it when I was dead though, so I had to stop.

I miss my coffin. It was nice to go away without going anywhere. Getting older sucks sometimes.

Most of the time.

Button down from the top. One-two-three-four-five-six. Don't like six as much as five. Too many factors. Prime is better.

"Frederick. I'm waiting, honey." She calls me honey when she doesn't want to sound annoyed with me. She doesn't know that I can hear the steel in her voice.

Slide my pajama bottoms off, pointing my toes so that my slippers stay on. Don't want one of them to fall off. It would take a long time to get downstairs if I have to start everything over again. Mom isn't a very patient waiter.

I know that *waiter* is the wrong word for someone who

is waiting for you to get dressed to go to the police. *Waiter* is the noun used to describe someone who waits on tables, which doesn't mean standing around wondering where you are. Words are interesting to me, but most of the time they don't make sense. I want to live someplace where words say exactly what they mean. Most English words mean whatever the person talking wants them to mean, which a lot of the time isn't what the person listening to the person talking *thinks* they mean. I don't think many people who speak English actually read the dictionary regularly so that they know what they're talking about. I read the dictionary every day, but most of the time it doesn't help.

"Frederick! We're going to be late!" Steel sharpening. Have to hurry up so I don't get cut, and pieces of me bleed out onto the floor.

Pants on fast, left leg first. Pajamas under my pillow. Check the bed for wrinkles one last time. Sit on my chair that sits beside my dresser that has my sock drawer in it. Isn't it funny that I sit on a chair that sits on the floor even though it isn't sitting at all? Take out a fresh pair of socks. Left slipper off. Left sock on. Left shoe on. Always left first. Left right, left right. First my bed is in the army, now my feet!

"Coming Mom!" I finally remember to answer her so she won't get too upset.

Now that we're sitting here in the police station with an officer who asks too many questions, I've figured out that my mom was already too upset before we even got in the car.

It's only going to get worse.

I have a bad feeling I know what this is about.
The police want answers that I'm not allowed to give.
Don't tell
Don't tell
Don't tell.

two

"It's okay, Fred. You don't have to be nervous. All I need is for you to tell me about Friday. Yesterday."

"Frederick," my mom says very quietly as if my name embarrasses her, which wouldn't make sense because I assume she's the one who picked it.

Maybe my father picked it, and that's why my mom doesn't like it. She doesn't like my dad much because he left us when I was a baby and my mother was a younger version of herself. My mother says that I had nothing to do with my father's decision to leave, but you have to admit the timing of it is somewhat suspicious. I don't know where he went, and I don't care. I don't miss him. You can't miss something you never had—that's what my mother says anyway.

I think you can miss something you *wish* you had though.

I don't wish I still had my father. I wish I had a movie

theater. My very own movie theater where I decide what movie is going to be played and when it's going to happen.

When I was little, I discovered that when you watch a movie on a giant movie-theater screen, it's so big that it's impossible to focus on anything else. If you focused hard enough, you could disappear right into the screen with the actors. Once you're in there they wouldn't be actors anymore. They'd be the real people and everyone on the outside would be the actors.

If I had my own movie theater I could choose where and how to live my life, and no one could tell me that I was doing it wrong because they would all be on the outside looking in, and I would be on the inside looking out, a thousand times bigger than they are.

But I don't have my own movie theater. I go to movies sometimes, but now that I'm older, it's harder to figure out how to get out of my seat and into the movie. My mind is too full of other things now to let me focus it enough.

Getting older sucks.

My mother doesn't like it when I say *sucks*. She said it's just rude and doesn't actually mean anything. I'm fully aware that it's rude and I know what it means—which has nothing to do with getting liquid out of a container using a straw. At least not in this context. My mother says that I'm too old to use words like *sucks* and that I should always strive to be pleasant.

Striving to be pleasant sucks. And not having my own movie theater sucks.

I like the word *sucks*. It's short and you can say it loudly when you're angry and it sounds like a feeling. You can make the Ss really long and push the K right into the back of your throat.

S-s-s-ucK-s-s-s.

Makes me feel like a pissed-off snake.

I used to say *angry* but now I say *pissed off* because I'm older. People my age say *pissed off*. It means the same thing as *angry* but it feels angrier. If you shout it, everyone knows you mean it.

I'M PISSED OFF! You have to say it loud enough so you can hear the exclamation point.

"What?" The policeman says to my mother, sounding pissed off but trying not to. I wait for my mother to tell him that it's rude to say *what* instead of *excuse me*.

"He prefers to be called Frederick. It might make this go more easily."

"Oh. *Fred*erick is it? All right then, Frederick, let's go through this quickly, so we can get you out of here. Okay?" He says my name with too much emphasis on the first syllable. Emphasis is important in a name. I prefer that all syllables receive the same respect. I consider telling him this just so we understand each other better, but the look on my mother's face tells me no. I can't always read my mother's face, which seems to get me in trouble a lot, but sometimes her thoughts are written pretty clearly. Right now the words I'm reading are *pay attention*. What else is new?

Actually lots else is new, but now isn't the time to think about that.

"Okay," I answer, even though it really isn't. Sometimes lies are easier than truth.

ROBERT

"So, all I want you to do is tell me about your Friday. What you did, where you went, who you talked to."

"First, I turned off my alarm clock."

The officer shakes his head. Wrong answer on the very first question. If this was a test I'd already be flunking it.

"No, *Fred*erick. I don't need that kind of detail. Okay? Just…tell me who all you talked to on Friday."

"I talked to Microman a bit on the computer before I left for school."

"His friend Robert," my mother adds to my answer, which is something I do not like her to do. I'm not a math problem that she needs to add onto. She doesn't do it as much now as she used to, but I think even once is too often. I have my own answers. She doesn't know what they are and shouldn't be giving them out to people.

This time she's mostly right though. I'm fairly certain that Robert is my friend. We play games and talk on the computer. He helps me notice the math teacher. We went to a movie together once. He is better at social skills than I am, but I am better at math than he is, so it balances out. He calls himself Microman when we are on the computer together. He likes to think about all of the tiny pieces of matter that go together to make everything in the physical world. He always says that he wishes he could be microscopic, so that he could disappear inside of things and figure out how they work. I don't know why I said it out loud though. It's supposed to be a name you see but don't hear.

"Mrs. Barry, I need you to let Frederick answer for himself, if you're going to stay here with him. I understand his…

special needs are the reason you're here, but you really have to respect the process. Please." He tacks on the polite word as an afterthought.

Please and *thank you.* Say them whether you mean them or not. That's what my mother taught me. It's polite to say them. Even if you don't mean them. Thanking people, whether you're feeling thankful or not. And *please.* What does it even mean? You ask for a glass of juice and your mother says "Say please." Why? If you don't say *please* you don't get the juice. That's why. "I need a cup of juice" is a clear statement of need. It doesn't sound rude to me. Why do you need *please* added on? It's just an extra word and it doesn't add any meaning to the sentence. I think it's rude to say something you don't mean.

I don't think the officer really meant *please.* I think he meant *So, shut up* but decided *please* sounded more polite.

"Fine. Yes, I understand. Thank you for letting me be here with him." I don't think my mother really means *thank you* either. The words are there, but her voice doesn't sound very thankful. It sounds pissed off.

"Microman?" The officer shakes his head, looking down at a notepad sitting in front of him. I'm surprised to see him using a notepad. You would think that he would use a laptop or a tablet. I wonder what number his pencil is?

"He's just a…friend. He's not in my grade, and I don't really talk to him at school much."

"Oh. Well, I'm asking you about people you actually talk to at school. *Did* you talk to anyone once you got to school on Friday?"

"No."

"You didn't talk to anyone? No one talked to you?"

"Oh. Someone talked to me. I didn't talk back."

"Who was that?" Officer Smith has his pencil poised to write down the name I give him, as if it is very important information.

"Peter Murphy."

"This Peter, is he a friend of yours?"

"No. Not a friend. He's a Despiser."

Another word I shouldn't be saying out loud. Talking to the police sucks.

"A what?" His pencil is still up above the notepad waiting for something to write.

"A Despiser. He despises me. He's not my friend." I shrug my shoulders like it's obvious. I do this because it *is* obvious. What else would a Despiser be?

I don't think the word *Despiser* is in the dictionary. I should look it up though, just in case. It's a word I think I made up. A category. Despisers are different from Haters. More intense. The Despisers are kids like Peter Murphy and Brian Jackson and Jimmy Dames and Janet Ellison and Suzanne Mallroy and Karen Brittan and Ellen Krisdale and Ally Schuster and a bunch of other kids.

"What did he say to you?" Officer Smith doesn't ask me *why* Peter despises me. My mother's mouth has popped open a little, and I suspect she wants to ask a question, but she's afraid if she talks she'll be kicked out of this very small room, which is mostly made of glass so everyone can stare at us when we're talking.

"I don't remember exactly. Nothing important. He just likes to call me names that aren't mine and stuff. No big deal." I shrug again to show him that it's no big deal. Shrugging works for lots of different things you might want to say when you are tired of using your mouth.

I'm lying to Officer Smith. I know that you aren't supposed to lie, especially not to police officers, but I do it anyway. I don't like sharing the things that Peter Murphy says.

"Hey, Gayboy. I'm talking to you. Are you a deaf homo or just a retarded one?" He pushes me lightly on the shoulder, hard enough for me to feel, but not hard enough for anyone else to see.

"Hey, Fagface. I asked you a question!" He pushes me again, harder this time.

"Peter. Leave him alone. You seriously need to find something else to do to besides picking on people." I'm still walking without looking at anyone, but I know the second voice. It belongs to Eileen Campbell. She's a Helper. Helpers feel sorry for people like me and get involved a lot to try to help us. Helpers aren't friends any more than Despisers are, but they don't hurt as much. Despisers sometimes listen to Helpers. They aren't afraid of them but Helpers like Eileen use loud voices so that the Despisers will be noticed and get in trouble. Sometimes it works and other times it makes everything a hundred times worse because the Despiser gets pissed off and takes it out on me later.

"Eileen, you're such a dyke. You should mind your own business."

"Yeah, well so should you. Oh, look there's Mr. Thoms…"
Mr. Thoms is our VP and he's extremely strict. Even Despisers
try to avoid going to his office.

"Whatever. You're both losers. Seriously pathetic gay little
freak-faced losers."

"At least your vocabulary's getting bigger. Homophobe
freak!" Eileen kind of shouts this down the hall at Peter's back.
I'm still walking, looking down at my feet and trying to encour-
age them to move faster so that I'll be in my next class before
Eileen catches up to me. Helpers like her try to talk to me and
get me to thank them for helping. I don't want to say thank
you even though I suspect my mother would tell me that it is
the polite and therefore right thing to do.

Saying thank you to Eileen is just like having to say it to
my grandmother when she buys me another Archie comic when
I would really prefer X-Men. I'm not supposed to be honest and
tell my grandmother that I really prefer X-Men. I'm supposed
to pretend that I am really happy with an Archie comic that
my grandmother wasted her money on. This is not counted as
lying because it is polite, according to my mother. Lying comes
in categories just like the kids at school.

I don't want to thank Eileen because I don't want her help.
I want everyone to leave me alone. Like the Avoiders do.

The Avoiders are the kids who act like they think that
whatever I have is catching. They avoid any kind of contact with
me at all. If they have to walk past me in the hall, they try to
make themselves smaller so they won't accidentally touch me.
If they have to walk towards me in the hall, they always look

down at their shoes so they don't have to look at me. I think that Avoiders are my favorite other people.

Gay. Retard. Fag. Fairy. Loser. Homo.

Words that mean different things depending on whose mouth they come out of.

Peter Murphy always calls me Gay or a Fag. I know what he means when he uses those words. He means that he thinks that I am a homosexual and that he thinks that being a homosexual is a bad thing. I know what a homosexual is. It's someone who wants to be with a person who is the same gender as he or she is. Not just be with them but fall in love with them and have sex.

I don't know why Peter thinks that I am a homosexual. I don't think I'm any kind of sexual yet. I don't want to have sex with anyone. I don't know for sure if this is normal or not for someone my age. My mother tried to talk to me about sex a couple of times. She tried to tell me about urges I was going to have and how normal they were going to be and how I had to understand the rights and wrongs about how to deal with those urges. I didn't like talking to her about urges so she bought me a book. I thanked her for the book but I didn't really need it because we had already talked about all of those same things in health class in school.

I suppose that Peter and his friends think that I am homosexual because one of the only people I ever talk to at school is Robert, although I don't really talk to him very much because he's in grade twelve and is in a club that meets at lunch time and I don't like clubs. Robert talks to me online more than at school. He doesn't call me names. He knows I'm smart like he is in most things and smarter in math. I think that makes us friends. I don't think it makes us homosexuals because I am not in love with Robert and I don't think I want to have sex with him.

I'm not in love with anyone yet.

I don't quite understand why Peter and his friends have decided that being a homosexual is a bad thing. So bad that they use it as the one horrible thing they choose to say to the people that they hate. Maybe Despisers just like to hate so much that they will find any excuse to do it.

I wonder if I will ever be in love with someone? Or if anyone will ever be in love with me?

three

We're taking a break from questions. We haven't really done very many but the officer seems tired. Tired in that same way my mom seems sometimes when we try to have a conversation. She says I'm hard to have a conversation with because I don't keep to the topic. I'm never sure what the topic actually is so it's kind of hard to keep to it.

I'm pretty sure I know what the topic is supposed to be today but Officer Smith seems to have trouble finding his way to it. He just keeps asking me vague questions that circle around the real reason I'm here. He has apparently watched too many cop shows on TV and has decided that the best way to elicit a confession from me is to keep going around and around until I'm so dizzy that I can't help but spill my guts to him.

Circles seem rather useless as an interrogation tool. They don't have a beginning or an end. They just keep going 'round and 'round without a purpose or direction.

My mom and the officer are having a conversation outside the door. The door isn't closed all of the way and I can hear them. I know what the topic of *their* conversation is. Me.

"I wish you would tell me what this is all about. I could help you get through to him if I knew what you were looking for." My mother is trying to sound calm but her voice is shaky like it gets when she is really angry with me but trying not to show it.

"Mrs. Barry, you have to let me do this my way. I'm just looking for him to volunteer some information."

"I can see that. But Frederick sees the world…differently than other kids. You have to be direct with him if you want to know something."

"Because of his…what is it he has? Autism?"

"His diagnosis is Asperger's but he doesn't really like me to talk about it. He has trouble with social cues most of the time but really it's not that different than talking to any other child. Just…be clear and direct with him."

"I will be as clear as I can be without doing any leading. I just need him to cooperate."

"This *is* him cooperating."

My mom laughs a little. Very little. More of a snort than a laugh. Officer Smith doesn't. They're talking about me as if I'm not here. Maybe I'm not. Maybe I'm just a figment of all of our imaginations. A shadow on the wall. Or a space alien with powers of invisibility. I would love to be one of those! I used to pretend that I was invisible when I was a kid. If I didn't pay attention to anyone in the room, they couldn't pay attention to me. I became a piece of the wind, a breeze at the window that no one could see unless the curtains moved.

Maybe I'm invisible now. Maybe I can just get up out of this chair and head out of this place. I don't like it here. I don't like answering questions that don't have any point to them. I don't like that my mother is talking about me in loud tones that bounce off the walls and hit me in the face.

I push the chair back silently. Invisibility works best in silence, although it's kind of fun to make noise when you're invisible because it freaks out the visible people. Today is not a day for fun though. I stand up slowly so that nothing on me creaks. I take in a breath through my nose because it's quieter than my mouth. I hold it to make me lighter so my feet don't make a sound. I open the door and walk carefully behind my mother and the policeman, making sure I don't touch them. They probably wouldn't notice even if I did. They would blame the wind.

My mother and the officer are still talking. It's easy to get behind them and move beyond them.

"Hey, where do you think you're going?"

I stop dead. That's a weird expression when you think about it. Stop dead. Dead means you're not alive any more. If you stop without dying, don't you stop alive?

I stop alive. I guess today isn't my day to be an invisible alien. Bad timing. I hate when that happens.

"Frederick? Honey? Didn't we ask you to wait in the room?"

"No."

"No? What do you mean by that?" The officer looks at me and then at my mother. He doesn't know what *no* means? I wonder what you have to do to become a police officer anyway—be able to breathe?

"I mean the opposite of yes. A negative response to a question. As in, no you didn't ask me to wait in the room."

They both just look at me for a second. Well, actually seven seconds according to the second hand on my diver's watch. I don't go diving but I found this watch at a garage sale and it still worked and it had lots of interesting dials and extra features on it so I bought it. Mostly I bought it because it only cost me four dollars. I like garage sales. So many treasures that other people actually throw away, thinking they're garbage. They let you buy stuff from them for almost nothing. Almost nothing. Why did I think that? My mother says it sometimes. I think it's a strange combination of words. You either have something or you have nothing. How can you have almost nothing? If you have almost nothing than you have something. If you have almost something, then you have nothing.

"Well, it was implied. And I'm telling you now. You wait in the room until I give you permission to leave. Understand?" The officer stares at me, leaning forward so he's sliding into my personal space. I close my eyes and concentrate on shallow breathing. It's hard to breathe when someone comes into my personal space. They take my air away into their own lungs and don't leave enough for me.

"Frederick? Did you hear Officer Smith?"

I nod because I can't talk when someone takes my air. Officer Smith steps back and I can breathe again so I open my eyes. He's looking at me and shaking his head.

Back we go into the very small room with glass walls. They look like windows but they don't open. I would guess that would define the difference between a wall and a window. "You make a better door than a window." Robert says that if I accidentally stand between him and something he wants to see. If I was a glass door, he wouldn't say it.

Once we're in the room, we sit on opposite sides of the small table that sits in the middle of the floor space. I don't know if it's the exact middle because I have nothing to measure it with but there appears to be close to an equal amount of space on each side. The important thing is that the table is sufficiently wide to keep Officer Smith from violating my air space.

Smith. That sounds like a pseudonym.

"Hey, Frederick, are you with me?"

I nod my head without looking at him.

"Can you look at me, please?"

He says *please*, but he really isn't trying to be polite.

When I was smaller, I didn't really like to look into other people's eyes. It hurt when they tried to get inside me through my eyes, so I usually kept mine looking down at the floor. People's feet didn't hurt as much as their eyes. At least not until I got to middle school and some of the guys at school decided to kick me whenever no one else was looking. That hurt, too.

Look at me, Frederick. Let me see your eyes, Frederick. Eye contact, please, Frederick. Look at me, look at me, *look at me*.

Pay attention. Pay attention. Pay attention.

I finally figured out how to shield myself from other people's eyes even though it still seems like I'm looking at them. I can point my eyes in the right direction, but blur out the image so that I don't let them inside. No one knows I can do this except Robert. Even my mother doesn't know. Robert only knows because he does it sometimes too.

I look up at the officer, keeping all my shields in place.

"When is the last time you saw Angel Martinez?" He finally decides to ask me a direct question. The one that I was expecting but dreading at the same time. I was right. She is the topic of this ridiculously round conversation. The question comes at me sooner than I thought it would and takes me a little off guard, like a soldier who stops to look at a flower, instead of keeping his eye on the enemy line.

"I don't know exactly." Not a lie. I don't know *exactly*.

"Did you talk to her on Friday?" His voice is louder now.

I did talk to her but I can't tell him that, even though that part isn't actually the secret. But if I tell him the non-secret part, then the secret part might accidentally attach itself, like an unwelcome virus slipping into my e-mails.

She talked to me that day.

Which Officer Smith likely already knows, but instead of just saying so, he just keeps spinning everything around.

"Frederick. Do you know where Angel Martinez is?"

The words come out slowly and clearly. All of his circles are suddenly gone and we are heading straight forward. I can see the destination ahead of me, and it isn't a good place to be going.

Maybe circles aren't so bad after all.

"No." My voice is not loud at all, but he can hear me.

This is true. I don't know for sure where she is right at this exact moment. She can't be where she's supposed to be, or I wouldn't be here.

"Did you know that she's missing?"

I shake my head. My mother gasps a little, like you do when you first come up out of the water after holding your breath for a long time.

I'm not lying. I didn't know she's *missing*. According to her, no one was going to actually ever think that.

That was the plan.

Me sitting in a police station was so *not* the plan.

"Fred. I need you to look at me now." I can feel him leaning toward me across the table. I'm feeling shaky, and I don't trust my shields right now so I drop my head down onto my arms, like our teacher used to make us do in grade school when she was tired of us.

"If you have any information about Angel you have to tell me. Her parents don't know where she is. I've been told that you were the last person anyone saw talking to her on Friday."

I keep staring down at the table. I wonder how often they clean the furniture here? I can imagine colonies of bacteria marching around, organizing themselves into battalions, ready to attack anyone foolish enough to touch the tabletop. Imagining germ armies is better than answering Officer Smith. I don't know what words would end this conversation so that I can go home and try to figure out what to do next. She said it would be easy. She said no one would get upset. She said it would work out fine.

She said I wouldn't get into trouble if I helped her, so long as I kept my mouth shut.

She told me over and over and over.

Don't tell
Don't tell
Don't tell.

four

When I'm online, I call myself Kaleidoscope. I had one when I was a kid. I used to look at it for hours. I loved the way I could swirl the colors together. It looked so random and uncontrolled, one color swishing its way onto another until they blended together making something new. Except that it wasn't random or uncontrolled at all. All of the pieces had to be arranged in perfect order so that when you twisted the piece at the end, the right colors would find each other and swirl together perfectly.

Everyone thinks that my mind is too full of thoughts that swirl together and come out in the wrong order. That I daydream or fade out or lose focus or forget to pay attention. That I'm disordered or random sometimes. They even came up with an unwanted title for me. ADD. Attention Deficit Disorder. They think I don't have enough attention.

I have plenty of attention. The kind you don't have to pay

for. It's all free, and it's all mine. I have thousands of thoughts in my head. The average person has something like sixty thousand thoughts a day. I guess I'm not average because I have a hell of a lot more than that. My mother doesn't like it when people use the word *hell*.... She calls it blaspheming. I don't care. It's a good word when you want some emphasis. H-E-double hockey sticks. That's what Mom calls it. Lame.

My thoughts are not random. They mean something to me. I have them all organized into my filing system in my mind. The problem is that no one seems to understand my system. They don't see the dots between my thoughts that connect them to make complete and total sense.

Even my mom, who loves me the most, according to her, doesn't understand that my thoughts are all laid out clearly, their colors carefully chosen so that when they swirl together, they make new thoughts.

Thinking about kaleidoscopes is not random right now because I'm thinking about Angel and how she found me in the library the first time.

The library is a really good place to hide. If you sit way at the back in the reference book section, you don't see anyone else at all. I can use my phone to message Robert without having to actually talk to him out loud at school.

Microman:
So much math homework tonite. Sucks.

Kaleidoscope:
Already done.

Microman:
U suck!

Kaleidoscope:
Still have science lab to write up. Doing it now.

Microman:
U should come to computer club instead.
Library is boring.

Kaleidoscope:
Computer club is boring.

Microman:
U never gave it a chance. Come now.

Kaleidoscope:
Not today. Busy.

Microman:
Always busy. U should try having fun sometimes.

Kaleidoscope:
Science labs are fun.

"That's a cool name. I love kaleidoscopes. You hardly ever see them anymore, do you? I had one when I was little. I loved mashing up all the colors and making new patterns."

The voice startles me so much that I almost drop my phone. The fact that someone has found me in the library surprises me so much that it takes all of my words away. The fact that someone is reading my private name over my shoulder pisses me off so much that I almost throw my phone at her. But I can't move because she's so close to me that's she's completely invaded my personal space. I close my eyes and concentrate on shallow breathing.

"Hey, Kal! Are you okay?"

I nod because I can't talk without my air. She steps away from my back and moves to my front, far enough away that I can breathe again, so I open my eyes. She's looking at me and shaking her head a bit. I guess she thinks I'm weird. Lots of people think I'm weird. I don't care.

"Sorry about that. I guess I surprised you. I didn't mean to be rude. I've just noticed you around a bit, and you seem kind of nice. I don't know that many people here, so I figured I'd just say hi or whatever." She smiles at me. I have no idea what she wants from me so I just stare at her.

"Hey, Kal, don't look so scared. I only bite guys on Fridays. And today's Thursday."

"Kal? My name isn't Kal. It's Frederick." I manage to get the words out and make sure to say it clearly with all of its syllables intact. She just laughs.

"Seriously? Well, I like Kal better. Suits you. The whole

Kaleidoscope thing is cool you know? I love them. When I was little I loved how the colors seemed so crazy and random but really weren't. Totally cool."

I look at her in surprise. How could she know that?

"My name is Angel. How totally lame is that? I tried to get my parents to change it to Angela when I was a kid, but they told me that Angel is a beautiful name in Spanish and lots of kids are named that in Mexico where my dad was born. I tried to tell them that we don't live in Mexico, and that I don't speak Spanish, but they don't care. I get teased a lot…people telling me I'm no angel and crap like that. Asking to see my wings. I call myself CC online though. CC stands for Chubby Cherub. On account of the size of my big butt." She laughs again and kind of wiggles her bum around. I try not to look but it is really quite big and fills up my field of vision.

I'm surprised to hear her talking about her size in that way. My mother always tells me that people don't like to talk about their size, especially if it's big, and that you must never refer to a person's weight unless you are telling them that they lost some. She says that's always a compliment, although that doesn't make sense to me. I have noticed that most people are very unhappy if they think they have too much weight. I have always been very skinny on account of my hyperactive metabolism. My mother often says she wishes she could borrow it from me for a while, which I know is a joke because it's a physical impossibility.

Anywhere you see advertising the message seems to say that skinny is the best thing to be, and that being anything else is something to be ashamed of. Seems strange to me. Who cares what your body looks like? It's just your container, like a cereal box. I think most cereal boxes are silly, with overly bright colors creating confusing pictures that don't actually tell you anything about what is inside. But it doesn't matter how weird the outside of the box is, the inside can still be filled with vitamin-enhanced nutritious morsels that also taste really good. I think cereal is pretty close to the perfect food, even though I don't like the containers it usually comes in.

When I first met Angel, she seemed different from most girls. She seemed to make fun of herself and everyone else. Nothing seemed to bother her.

When I first met Angel that's how it seemed.

"Frederick? Are you awake?" Officer Smith taps his pencil on the table close to my hands. It startles me, and my eyes accidentally open up and look right at him. His eyes are staring into mine, trying to get past my defences and inside my mind where he'll find Angel. I'm not properly prepared to defend against his ambush and he almost gets through. I have to quickly close my lids again to get under control so that I can regain my focus.

"Hey, you keep your eyes open. I'm not that ugly!" He kind of laughs. My mother does too, although hers is the totally fake kind that people use when they're pretending to laugh at someone else's stupid joke.

Deep breath. Concentrate. Keep the focus in. Keep him out.

I open my eyes. My mother smiles at me. I think it's one of her encouraging smiles. She has a lot of different smiles that she uses to try to tell me different things, even though she knows that reading faces is not one of my strongest skills. I prefer to read books.

"Are you okay?" He asks me, still trying to look into my mind. My defences are back up and working so he can't see anything but my irises, my pupils, and the whites of my eyes. Everything else is safely hidden from view.

"He seems to have a lot of trouble focusing on the questions. He keeps drifting away here. That part of the disorder?" He looks at my mother, who looks at me. I'm not sure what he's referring to, but then again, I don't know how long I was thinking about Angel and whether I missed some questions or not. I do know I don't like him talking about me to my mother when I'm sitting right here.

"I'm not disordered. I have everything exactly where I want it to be. It's the outside that's disordered, not me."

He looks at me like I just started speaking in a foreign language. Maybe I should have said it in German. I've been teaching it to myself using the Internet. I like German. It's a very structured language and much of it sounds like English.

"All I want is for you to answer the questions when I ask them. Can you do that?" he asks.

Nein, Officer Dummkopf.

I'm looking down at the table so he can't see me smile with my eyes. I wish I could call him Officer Dummkopf out loud, but my mother wouldn't be too happy with me if I did. I wonder what the German word is for officer? I'll have to look it up when I get out of here.

I can hear Officer Dummkopf breathing. I had an upper respiratory infection once and it made me breathe in a strange way that I didn't like. I sounded like someone else, and it scared me. I don't like to be sick. It makes my body feel like I don't own it anymore, and I don't know how to be. I wonder if Officer Smith has some sort of respiratory issue because his noise is loud. So loud that I can't hear my mother, although I know she must be breathing also. She is likely worrying, too, because she always worries when she thinks I am going to make a social mistake. That's what she calls them. *Social mistakes*. It means I've said or done something that other people think is inappropriate for some reason that makes no sense to me but makes perfect sense to Mother. She never gets angry with me because she knows I don't do it on purpose. So she calls them mistakes.

What she doesn't know is that sometimes I do it on purpose. Sometimes it's easier to pretend you don't know the right way to act. It makes the other people leave you alone faster. Sometimes.

I look up and he's staring at me with hard eyes. I look over at my mom, whose eyes are much softer but definitely looking worried, even to me. I guess the socially appropriate thing here is to respond out loud, in English, and I imagine that *no* isn't the answer he's looking for.

"I'll try, but sometimes I have problems with remembering. Part of my disorder."

I cross my fingers when I say the last word so it doesn't count. He looks rather pleased that I admitted to my "disorder." Probably thinks he's going to cure me.

I'm not lying. Even though I am *not* disordered, I do sometimes have trouble with my memory. I can remember lots of kinds of things, especially if they're things I've seen on TV or heard in class on the days that the teacher says something interesting. Facts go into my mind and like to stay there. I have thousands of bytes of information in my head that I keep organized in a detailed filing system.

But there are some things that I seem to have great difficulty holding on to, like all of the so-called social rules that my mother and teachers have been drilling into me since I was small, making little holes in my mind and poking around in there until I feel like I want to run away screaming. Social rules are illogical and random. My filing system doesn't have an *Illogical and Random* folder.

"What if I told you that other students say they saw you with Angel Martinez on Friday?" He throws the question at me like a football, hoping I'll fumble the answer. I hate football.

"Other students say lots of things about me. They are often not true."

When I was in grade school, Billy Waters told the teacher that I was the one who wrote *F you* on the blackboard. Except it wasn't just the F but the whole swear word. Well, almost the whole word. It was spelled without the C, which should have made it obvious that it wasn't me because I was the best speller in the class. I knew that Billy was the one who did it, and lots of other kids knew it too. The teacher started interrogating us. Most kids said they didn't know anything about it. Five kids said it was me. No one said it was Billy. Five kids voted for me, even though I didn't do it. Backwards popularity. I had detention for a whole week and my mother told me that this was more serious than a social mistake. I didn't bother telling her I didn't do it. Too much evidence against me.

"Did the teacher say she saw them?" My mother's voice is soft, like she wants to be heard but is a bit afraid of speaking out loud.

"Mrs. Barry, I warned you. You can't speak during this, or you will have to leave. This is your last warning."

I have a sudden urge to laugh, but I swallow it hard. It just sounds so funny to hear my mother being given a last warning. That has always been one of her favorite things to say to me. "Turn off that computer right now. This is your last warning." "Get dressed for school right now. This is your last warning." "Turn your light out. This is your last warning." Except that she never says what will happen next, if I don't do what she says. How is that a warning at all, if it doesn't come with consequences?

Officer Smith is warning my mother though. She will have to leave me here alone, if she doesn't behave. That is a consequence for me. I would rather not be alone with Officer Smith.

"When is the last time you saw Angel Martinez?" Officer Smith is still talking in a straight line.

His smile is gone and he is staring at me. The question seems very important to him, and I know I should answer quickly, but I'm trying to remember exactly what I already said. My memory usually acts like a pair of scissors for my own words, cutting them into manageable pieces, so I can store them where they belong. But I can't find them now. Nothing is working right today.

"Frederick. Before you get yourself in deeper here, I think you should know that we had a chat with the supervisory teacher from the classroom you eat lunch in. A Ms. Belton. She isn't your usual teacher I know, but she did remember seeing you and Angel there together. Talking together. Does that jog your memory?"

I look at him in surprise. If this was a TV show, he would have withheld that information just in case I lied, so he could use it against me. Or something like that.

Jog my memory. Such a strange expression. Jogging your mind instead of your feet.

"Yes." I don't even know what I'm saying yes to. Lying is very messy, and I'm starting to get buried in my own pile of crap. Gross.

"Yes you ate lunch with her?"

"Yes, I guess so."

"So you ate lunch and had a conversation with her on the day she disappeared. You remember that now?"

"Yes." I remembered it before too.

"As far as we know, you were the last person to see her. She didn't arrive at her next class. No one has seen her since."

He's staring at me. I don't say anything because no one asked me a question.

"Frederick. Do you know where Angel went after her lunch with you?"

"No." The answer comes out quickly because it's true. I don't know where she went. I know where she was *planning* to go, but I don't know if that's where she actually went.

"And do you know where she is now?"

"No." I make eye contact with him so he knows it's the truth.

He stares at me for another moment. I can see more questions in his eyes, but he decides not to ask them for some reason. He looks at my mother, instead.

"If either of you thinks of anything that could help us to find her, you need to call or come in right away. Frederick was the last person we know of who talked with her. He might remember something that could help us. Any little thing could be important. Time is of the essence here, so call anytime."

"Certainly. We'll do anything we can to help, right Frederick?"

"Right."

"Oh, and Mrs. Barry?"

"Yes."

"You need to stay available. In case we have more questions."

"Of course."

"Frederick. You need to try to remember anything you can. We're hoping for the best, but your friend could be in serious trouble. Anything you know, or even just think you know, is important for us to hear. If you want to help her get found, you have to think hard about what she said to you that might be significant. And you have to tell us *everything*." He emphasizes the last word, giving it all four syllables to stress its importance.

I nod. Nodding one's head is not as ambiguous as shaking. It most often means yes, but it can also mean you're considering something the other person has said. Either way, it's safer than using my voice.

My mother shakes hands with Officer Smith. I hurry out of the room, just in case he wants to shake my hand as well. I'm sure his germs are as unfriendly as his eyes.

I can't tell if I'm in trouble or not.

Am I doing something wrong? Should I tell them what I know?

Is Angel in serious trouble? She seemed so sure of herself and her plan. She said it was perfect.

But if it was perfect, why is she missing?

I don't know what to do now.

She told me what to do.

Or what not to do.

"Don't tell, don't tell, don't tell."

That's what she said. But she's not here.

Who do I listen to now?

five

We leave the station and Mom drives us home. I'm expecting her to finish Officer Dummkopf's interrogation, but the car is surprisingly silent. Our breath whooshes in and out. I imagine I can see it forming clouds in front of our faces and filling the car up with a fog that shields me from any more curiosity.

I'm glad my mother is quiet. I wish my head would shut up, too.

It's screaming at me. Telling me that all the Despisers are right; that I really am an idiot. How could I get involved in something that made me end up talking to a police officer at a police station? There, that sounds like a question that my mother should have asked me. I wonder why she is so quiet. Maybe it's not such a glad thing. Maybe she is really, *really* angry.

Sometimes, when my mother's anger becomes too much

for her to bear, she pushes it deep inside of herself where it sits and sucks away all of her words. She will look at me with quiet eyes that tell me I totally messed up, and she can't stand the thought of talking to me about it.

I like it better when she is just at a normal level of angry. Normal anger brings lectures and raised voices that travel right through me and don't leave any damage. Quiet anger is more dangerous. It sneaks inside me and hurts.

I can't tell if she's angry or not. Her face is busy looking out the windshield at the traffic. Her mouth isn't smiling or frowning. Just straight across the middle of her face, the misplaced radius of an imperfect circle.

When I was a little kid, I always drew faces that were perfectly round. That's how faces looked to me back then, long before anyone decided that I needed to look at cartoon pictures of feelings. I was very disappointed when I later discovered that faces are not round at all. In art class, the teacher makes us draw an oval as a starting point to drawing a human face. You start with the oval and then add and subtract lines until you create a nondescript image of a face that isn't any particular shape at all.

I like round faces better. I like the way most things looked to me as a kid better than the way they look now.

We're home now. Mother is still quiet. She turns off the ignition and starts to open her door without looking at me. She sits for a moment with her hand still on the door handle and the door barely open. Her eyes are staring straight ahead. She is completely still, like a perfectly chiseled stone replica of herself. I'm sitting still, too. I'm not sure if I'm supposed to get out of the car or not. I feel like I should wait for her for some reason, but I'm not sure why. I need some cues.

"Frederick. I need you to be totally honest with me." Her voice doesn't sound angry. It doesn't sound happy, either. There is something in there coloring it differently from usual, but I can't tell what it is.

"Yes." She still has her hand on the door. My hands are in my lap. I am staring out the windshield. I can feel my mother move, and I know she's looking at me. I know the right thing to do now would be to look at her, but I can't. I don't want to see her eyes. I don't want her to see mine.

"Do you know where that girl is?" *That girl.* She doesn't even remember her name! I'm in the biggest trouble of my life for someone who doesn't even have a name.

I know I have to answer fast. If I wait too long, she will think I am hiding something. I know this from experience, even though I have explained to her that sometimes it takes me a while to figure out what people want me to say. That my mind is like a computer screen typing the words as fast as I can think. I see them forming across my inner eyes, streams of information filling my brain. It's all in there, and I know where it all is. I just can't always find exactly what other people think they're looking for when they ask me a question.

"Frederick? I asked you a question. Are you hiding something from me?"

Now she's asked me two questions and I still can't find an answer that will work.

I can't tell. I swore I wouldn't. I can't break my oath.

But I can't lie to my mother. *Can* I?

"No." I say it quietly. I guess I can lie to my mother.

"You truly don't know where she is?"

"No." Not a full lie. A half-truth. Or maybe a quarter.

"Is this girl a friend of yours?"

I can still feel her looking at me. I wish she would get out of the car. It feels tight in here. I don't like tight places. Cars don't feel tight when they're moving, but when they're standing still like this they feel too small and cramped. I really want to get out of here.

Once, when I was about six or seven, my mother left me in the car while she ran into the store. She locked the doors so I would be safe. But she didn't understand about safe at all. She thought the dangers were outside of the car when they were really all inside. Closed in with the stale air that too many people had already breathed. Doors and windows laughing at me when I tried to get them open so I could find some new air so that I could breathe. I had to bang on the window with my fists, but they weren't hard enough, so I had to use my head. I had to hit it and hit it and hit it and hit it and hit it and hit it until suddenly it fell open.

I thought for a second that I had finally done it, but it was my mother. She grabbed me and yelled at me, asking what I was doing. Her eyes were crying. There were other people standing there looking at me but I couldn't see them very well. My eyes were filled with blood from the cut on my head.

My mother said I split my head open. That isn't really accurate. My actual head did not split. The skin on my forehead split. There is a lot of blood in the human head. I had to go to the hospital and get stitches. Sewing up a person like he is a pair of pants being hemmed is a strange thing.

I still have a scar on my forehead. It's pretty faded now but I can see it, if I look closely.

I look at the windshield. For just a second I feel like banging my head on it. Shake my brain around a bit to get my thoughts straight. Get my colors back in order. I don't do it though. My mother was so upset the last time that she made me go to a special doctor for months and months after. I didn't like the special doctor. He wasn't special to me. He was just in my face trying to make me see his world, instead of mine.

I was too young back then to explain what happened. And now, no one is really interested.

"Angel."

"Pardon?"

"Angel. Her name is Angel." *It's time to get out of the car now.*

"All right. Angel. Is Angel your friend?"

"She says so." *Right now. Out of the car.*

"Oh, I see." I'm not sure what she sees. Not much, or she would see that it's time to get out of the car now. Right now!

"Well, it's been a long morning. Let's each take some downtime and then see what I can find for lunch." She finally finishes opening her door. I grab mine and get out after her, fast before she can change her mind.

Downtime is one of my mother's favorite words. It doesn't really mean you have to lie down. It used to mean that when I was little, but now it just means that we each go to a separate place to be quiet and alone.

"All right. I might go out back then. Just for a little while." I chance a look at her. She looks at me hard and fast, catching my eyes and digging before I can get away.

"All right. I know that was very unpleasant for you. I hope that they find her soon. I'm sure she's all right, honey. Don't look so worried. She probably just went to a friend's house and forgot to call home or something."

That doesn't even make sense. How could someone go to a friend's for this long and forget to tell anyone? That's a pretty high level of forgetting.

"I'm not worried." The words come out before I realize that I picked the wrong ones.

"You're not? I thought she's your friend." My mother is trying to look inside, but I do a quick recovery and put up my shields before she gets in. I breathe in slowly, getting my mouth under control before I say something wrong again.

"I just mean, I'm sure she's fine. Angel's pretty tough."

"Oh? In what way?" My mother seems to have forgotten about downtime.

"Just…well, I guess I mean she can look after herself. Aren't we doing downtime?"

"Right. Okay. But I think we need to discuss Angel a little bit more after we eat. Deal?"

"Deal."

It's not really a deal at all though because we didn't shake on it, and my fingers are crossed.

My mother is a much better interrogator than Officer Dummkopf, and I will have to be ready for her.

I promised Angel. It's wrong to break a promise. But we didn't expect things to go this way. She was supposed to have called by now. She wasn't supposed to be missing.

No one was supposed to notice us talking in the Reject Room on Friday either.

We eat lunch in the Reject Room, which is what Ms. Jamieson's room is called. That's not one of my categories. Everyone calls it that. Especially the Despisers, which is interesting, considering that quite a few of them have to come here to see Ms. Jamieson for academic assistance. I don't come for that because I have strong academic skills in most subjects, except for the ones that shouldn't be in a school system, like gym. I hate gym because I am not athletically inclined and do not enjoy team sports of any kind. I would rather play chess if I have to play anything. I realize that chess would not exercise my body, but it does tone up my mind, which is the control center for my body. I tried to explain this to my guidance counsellor while asking for an exemption from gym class, but he didn't seem to understand me.

Math is basically my best subject in school except that not all of my math teachers like me much. I do most of my figuring out in my head, which apparently is a problem because math teachers aren't content with the correct answer. They are only content when the road you take to get the answer is the exact same road that everyone else takes. I like to go my own way. I end up at the same destination, and my way is usually better than the teacher's, but when I used to point that out during class, the teacher wasn't usually very appreciative.

My mother told me that teachers like to feel that they are right about things most of the time, even when they aren't. She actually admitted that most adults are like that. There's a presumption that age brings knowledge and that the younger you are, the less intelligent or wise you are. It's a bad presumption, and its very existence proves my point. People who presume they are more intelligent simply because they are older aren't intelligent enough to think outside of the box.

I think outside the box that other people have created. They've been trying to build it around me ever since I was born, making walls out of rules and expectations and words and more rules and more expectations and more words until the box has grown to giant proportions. I lived inside of the box for quite a while, trying to break it down but not able to figure out how. It took me a long time to realize that the best way to get out of the box was to pretend that I liked being inside of it, until people stopped trying so hard to keep me trapped in there. Once they let down their guards, my mind was able to find its way out.

I go to the Reject Room at lunch because it is part of my social assistance program. The school has brilliantly determined that I require assistance in the acquisition of social skills and one of the ways this is done is to keep me away from most of the student body at lunchtime. I eat with the other Rejects in Room 234. I assume they picked that room so that the rejects could remember the number sequence. There aren't many of us, and no one who eats in this room admits it outside of the four walls, so even if the officer went to school and tried to find someone who would say that I ate lunch with Angel, he wouldn't be able to. Rejects hide from everyone. They're like Avoiders, only they avoid themselves and everyone else.

I know that kids at school have me in the Reject category. There are different categories at school than in my head. There are the cool kids, the smart kids, the geeks, the fat kids, the jocks, the gay kids, the popular kids, the Haters like Peter, and the rejects like me. And probably lots of other categories. I fit into a few of them.

I don't have a category for myself in my head. For a category to have meaning, it really has to have more than one item in it. In my head, I am the only one like me. I don't need a category for myself.

I never did figure out what category Angel fits into. I know I was surprised the day I found her sitting in the Reject Room at lunch.

"Oh, well, it's just because I'm not used to the school yet. I heard that this place is a little quieter and friendlier than the cafeteria, so I thought I'd try it." Angel smiles at me when I get up the courage to ask her what she is doing in Ms. Jamieson's room. I don't really like asking people questions. I have a habit of asking the wrong ones, and people often don't like to answer me, or they answer me with words that I wasn't looking for. Angel doesn't mind my question though. Her smile seems real, the kind that just means she's being nice without any ulterior motives. I'm not sure about that though. She could just be pretending to be real, so I don't smile back. I'm thinking about her words. The Reject Room is definitely quieter than the cafeteria. Friendlier? No one has ever talked to me in here at all, except the one time that Robert came with me. He hated it here. He decided he would rather eat in the computer lab and risk getting in trouble for eating at the computers.

"Why did you come to this school?"

"Because my parents like to torture me."

"They torture you? How?"

"By moving. This is my sixth school, which isn't as many as some kids I know, but it still sucks. I'm only in grade ten, so I've only ever been in one school for two years. Hard to fit in when you keep leaving. What grade are you in?"

"I'm in grade eleven."

"Yeah? I totally thought you were my age."

"I'm sixteen but I'm small for my age and I have a young affect."

"Oh, yeah? Sounds like something some brilliant teacher said about you."

"Actually it was a not very brilliant psychologist."

She laughs, which surprises me. "A psychologist? Why? Are you nuts?" She looks at me with great interest. Maybe she's hoping I'll start foaming at the mouth or something.

"I don't think so, although I imagine some people around here do. No, I have trouble understanding social interactions. I have a label that someone gave me, but I don't want it so I don't talk about it." Don't know why I need a label to define myself. I know who I am. Giving me a label groups me together with many others who share a certain number of common characteristics that would then define me as a syndrome or a disorder rather than a person with a mind of my own. I don't want to be a syndrome, and I am far too orderly to be a disorder.

I just want to be me.

"You don't look that weird."

"I'm not very weird. Although lots of kids here call me that."

"Yeah. They call me names, too. Not the friendliest school I've ever been in. Not the worst, either, but close."

"What do they call you?"

"You don't really want to know, and it's not worth talking about. They're all full of crap anyway."

Since she said it's not worth talking about I don't say anything. We sit in silence for a few seconds. I like silence. It's feels comfortable, and I can wrap myself in it like the warm, soft sweater my grandma made for me that I still like to wear at home, even though my mother says it's so old I should throw it out.

The silence stretches out until we're both wrapped up in it, and I'm just wondering if the conversation is over so that I can leave, when she starts talking again. I've noticed that most people don't like silence as much as I do, always unraveling it into words that never feel as nice as my sweater does.

"Anyway, Kal, I'm pretty good at reading people, and I get the feeling that you'd never call me anything I don't like to be called, so maybe we could hang out a bit sometimes. Even though you're so much older and wiser than me."

She smiles again. It does look like a real one. I think. I still keep my smiles to myself. I don't give them out to just anyone, and I don't know her at all. She doesn't know me either, even though she thinks she can *read* me, because I'm very good at keeping my real self hidden.

She is right though. I never call people names. At least not out loud.

"I guess so." *I guess so* is a useful phrase. It doesn't really mean yes or no. It's nice and equivocal but it seems to make people think you've given them a real answer.

I forget for a second that she called me something I don't like to be called. Kal isn't my name. I think about reminding her of that, but she's already left the room by the time I finish the thought.

And now she's left more than just the room. She's gone, and I'm supposed to keep her secret because I promised.

She made me swear.

Don't tell

Don't tell

Don't tell.

six

I head out back to my thinking spot behind our house, which is a circle of trees that grow right out of a rock. My own personal Treehenge. That's a joke that I only ever told myself. I sit down on the smooth, cool rock with my back against the familiar roughness of the first tree. There's lots of sweet, fresh air out here, and I suck in as much as I can to help clear my head. I guess I do too good a job because all of a sudden, Angel comes whooshing in again to fill my mind up with her words.

I'm not sure how it happened, but after that first day in the Reject Room, Angel and I started eating lunch together every day. Well that's not accurate. Actually, I would eat and she would talk. And talk. And talk.

"Have you had sex with anyone besides yourself yet?"

"*What?*" I look around the room to make sure no one is

listening to us. I don't know why I bother. No one is looking at us or listening to us. We might as well be invisible.

"I said—"

"I heard you! Don't say it louder!"

"Well, what's the answer then?"

Angel's looking at me with a smile that is actually a grin. I didn't know what a grin was for a long time and how it was different from a smile. I read the definition, which just says it's a broad smile that shows the teeth. But I still couldn't imagine exactly why a grin needs its own word. A nice one I mean. Evil grins are easy to pick out. The Despisers excel at them. Spiked smiles that they try to impale you with.

Angel's grins are soft and silly around the edges. I know she's sort of teasing me when she grins but not in an evil way. When she grins at me, my mouth wants to smile, whether I tell it to or not, as if I've caught something from her, like a cold only less messy. Usually I have to remember to smile and then force the issue onto my face.

"I don't know what the answer is because I'm not sure what you mean by the question." I regret saying this as soon as I do it. I don't really want her to explain. Especially not here.

"You don't know what sex is? Intercourse? Copulation? Other smaller and ruder words that would get me in trouble?"

"Of course I know what it is! I just don't know what you meant by the last part."

"Oh, the *with anyone but yourself* part? I meant, have you had sex with anyone but your hand." She moves her hand up and down, curled around like a claw. Her grin is a little edgier now. It takes me an embarrassing minute before I realize she means masturbating.

I'm pretty sure that masturbation is not an appropriate topic to discuss with a young lady. Even Angel. My mother talked to me about it once, which was embarrassing enough. She told me it was something natural but very private. That it was all right to do it in the privacy of my bedroom, but it was not a subject for discussion. Which was confusing because she was discussing it while telling me not to, which was a contradiction.

I researched it after she left my room. According to the site I found parents used to tell their children that it would make them go blind. I'm not sure how anyone could have ever believed that there could be a causal link between self-stimulation and visual deterioration, but I guess kids will believe most things their parents tell them if they don't take the time to do the research.

When we had Sex Ed in sixth grade, the teacher talked about it. I didn't tell my mother, but I wondered what she would have thought about the teacher discussing a topic that isn't really appropriate for discussion. Not that we really discussed it much. The teacher talked about it and the girls giggled and the boys turned red and made stupid comments. I just tuned everyone out and thought about more interesting things.

"I don't think this is a subject for discussion."

"Come on, Kal, you sound like a teacher. Or worse, my mother. This is what friends talk about."

"It's private."

"That's the point. Friends are the only ones you can talk about private stuff with. Come on, we agreed. I'm the expert on friends, and you're the expert on pretty much everything else. Right?"

About two weeks after we met, Angel decided that she was going to be my friend because neither of us was doing very well in the finding friends department. I tried to find a polite way to tell her that I wasn't really looking for a friend. I told her I already have Robert but she just laughed and said that her father always says that variety is the spice of life. I told her that I've never been a big fan of spices because they burn my tongue, and she just laughed harder.

Somewhere between the spices and the laughing she decided that it was her job to teach me about friendship. Apparently we have an agreement now that I don't actually remember agreeing to. I know I have trouble remembering sometimes, but I seriously think that Angel has an overactive imagination, especially when it comes to things that she wants.

"I guess. I still don't like talking about it."

"It. You mean S-E-X. Come on, you can spell it at least."

"I can spell most things."

"I bet you can. I can't spell much of anything. You're still not answering me."

"No."

"No, you're not answering me, or no, you never had sex with anyone?"

"The second part."

"Oh. Me either. Why?"

"Why what?"

"Why have you never had sex with anyone? You're sixteen." She says it like I did something wrong. Sixteen is not particularly old not to have had sex yet. At least I don't think it is. I don't know why having sex is such a big deal anyway. TV shows seem obsessed with it. The kids at school talk about it all the time. I honestly have other things to think about. Most of the time.

And I definitely don't discuss it. Ever.

Not until now.

"I don't know. Why haven't you?" I don't really want to know. So I don't know why I asked her. You're supposed to ask questions when you're having a conversation. It's polite. I guess I'm just being polite. It's not always a good thing.

"First of all I'm only just turned fifteen, so it's not really as big a deal, although at my last school lots of my friends had already lost it by my age."

"Lost it?"

"Their virginity. That's what it's called when you do it the first time. You must know that. You do live in this world, right?"

"Of course, I know that. I just misunderstood you." I wonder why it's called losing your virginity. Losing something isn't usually a good thing. When you lose your wallet or your keys or your favorite comic, the natural reaction is to be upset. So, it's strange to me that everyone seems to think that having sex is such a good thing and then they call it losing your virginity. Shouldn't it be called finding something instead?

"Anyway, the second reason I haven't done it with anyone

yet is, well…kind of obvious." She looks at me and points to herself with the index fingers of both hands. I have no idea what she's doing. If I tell her that, she'll likely laugh at me, and the conversation will have to keep on going until someone hears us and gives the Despisers even more ammunition. Bullets of cruel information that'll come shooting out at me later.

"Oh, right." I nod, hoping it's the right thing to do. If I agree with her the conversation might end more quickly. I have found that most conversations can be ended pretty quickly and cleanly by pretending that you share the other person's point of view. Agreeing with people seems to make them happy.

Angel looks at me in silence, and I feel vindicated. I did it. I ended the conversation in an agreeable way before anyone else got an earful of incriminating information.

"That was a seriously shitty thing to say!" Her words are quiet but hard enough to smash the silence into a thousand pieces. Her eyes look as hard as her voice sounds. Her face does not look happy at all. Now what did I do?

I used to carry around a little book with cartoon pictures of people's faces in it showing different expressions. It was supposed to help me understand what faces say about feelings. Most people don't look much like cartoons though, so it never really did much good. Angel's face is quite round and is surprisingly like the cartoons, which makes me wish I had the book back so I could read her better.

I like cartoon faces. They remind me of the ones I used to draw when I was little. Maybe that's why I like Angel's face…except for right now when she looks like a pissed-off snake, her eyes all narrow and squinting at me like I'm a tiny rodent she wants for lunch. It doesn't take a book to tell me she's annoyed.

"What do you mean? I thought you wanted me to agree with you about things!" This friend thing can be very confusing. I need a rule book. I don't dare say that out loud though, or Angel will probably run off and write one for me.

"Oh, right. I want you to agree with me that I'm so fat no one will ever want to have sex with me." She puts her hands on her hips and frowns at me, sniffing a little as if she has a cold. I hope she doesn't. She's pretty close to me and her germs would have no trouble getting over here if she sneezed or coughed. Her eyes aren't squinting now, but they look a bit shiny. I think that I might have hurt her feelings, which means I have to apologize although I'm not exactly sure what I might have done wrong.

"I'm sorry. I didn't know that's what I agreed with."

"Seriously? You don't think that's the reason I'm still a virgin?"

"I've never thought about the reason you're a virgin. I don't think about things like that. And if I did think about it, I'd agree that it's because you are only fifteen." This time I'm agreeing for real.

"So, you don't think my body is too gross for someone to want to have sex with me?"

"You aren't *very* fat. Just moderately. Besides, I don't know what fat has to do with sex anyway." She looks at me for a second and then starts to laugh. She's laughing and sniffing and wiping snot off her face all at the same time. I don't think anyone would want to have sex with her right now, unless she washed her face first.

"Thanks Kal. I think you just totally insulted me and I'm pretty sure you have absolutely no idea how. Which is just so... you." She shakes her head. I lean back a bit so nothing splashes on me. I don't like other people's bodily fluids.

"I wasn't trying to insult you. I don't think there's anything wrong with your body. And I just thought sex was for love and that love doesn't have anything to do with looks. But I don't really know anything I guess." I shrug my shoulders. She looks at me for a moment.

"Maybe you do know everything after all." She smiles. I don't know what I said, but I guess it doesn't matter, so long as Angel thinks it was the right thing to say.

She gets up and leaves the Reject Room. No one notices her go.

No one notices us in the Reject Room most of the time. Except Ms. Jamieson, who always says hello when she's there.

She wasn't there that last day though. Friday. She was absent and there was a supply teacher, who didn't know our names. She didn't say hello. We were invisible to her.

So, who told the police that we were there together talking right before Angel disappeared?

How did I get in the middle of someone else's messed-up life?

Now it's my messed-up life, too.

I hate messes.

I never should have promised not to tell.

seven

"So…"

My mother looks at me expectantly. We've finished eating and are just sitting at the table. I'm staring down at my plate, which is still half full because I was too worried about my mother's interrogation to eat much.

"So what?" Pretending not to know what she wants isn't going to work this time, but I try it anyway.

"Tell me about Angel." Her voice is quiet but firm enough that I know she won't take excuses.

"She's just a girl at school who talks to me sometimes." *Pretty much true.*

"Why do the police think you might know where she is?"

"They are talking to everyone she knows. I think the officer said that. It's not just me." *Not true at all.*

"But you do know her." She either doesn't notice my lie or decides to ignore it.

"I already told you that."

"How well do you know her?"

I don't understand the question. How do you measure how well you know someone? What units would you use?

"I'm not sure what you mean."

"Look at me, Frederick." She puts her finger under my chin and tips my head up.

Pay attention. Pay attention. Pay attention.

We sit like that for a few seconds while she tries to get into my head and find Angel. She shakes her head a little and sighs.

"I mean, is she a close friend or just a casual one? Do you talk to her every day or just sometimes?" Multiple questions. I don't really understand the first ones so I try the second set.

"She talks to me most school days, and I talk back to be polite." Mom surprises me by laughing. She bends down and kisses me on the nose, releasing my chin at the same time. I resist the urge to wipe my nose off with my napkin because I know it would offend her. I'll wash my face after we leave the table.

"All right. I guess that's the best I'm going to get right now. You head up to your room. I'll clean up on my own. You've had a tough day."

I nod and push my chair back and head to the bathroom, where I wash my face and hands. I go up to my room and sit at my desk, trying to clear my head, but Angel sneaks in there and takes over again.

We're sitting in the library, in the back where I usually sit by myself. Robert is here too because he has to find some books for a research project, which means I had to introduce him to Angel, who, of course, asked him a whole bunch of questions about himself. I learned more about him in the last three minutes than in the whole two years I've known him. You're not supposed to talk in the library, but no one can hear us back here, so I don't bother reminding her about the rule. Angel's not a big fan of rules anyway.

"So what do you want to be when you morph into an adult?"

She's looking at me, so I assume that I'm being asked this question. I look at her for a second. I've had teachers who have asked the same basic thing…*what do you want to be when you grow up*? I've always thought it was a strange question. Won't I always just be me? Only maybe a bit taller?

"Me, only taller."

Angel looks at me and starts to laugh. She has a very loud laugh when she finds something particularly funny, a lot like the way I remember Santa Claus laughing in movies my mother used to make me watch, back when she was trying to make me believe in imaginary benefactors. If Angel doesn't lower her volume, we're going to get in trouble and the library monitor will kick us out. I've never been kicked out of the library.

"Sorry! That came out louder than I expected, but you are seriously funny sometimes. I want to be the same thing. Me, only taller. I've always suspected that I'm not actually overweight so much as underheight."

She starts laughing again, this time at herself. I don't know why she was laughing at me because I wasn't actually trying to be funny. *Seriously* funny. Sounds like an oxymoron. Robert is laughing, too, but I suspect that he is just doing it to be polite. He's better at social hypocrisy than I am.

"Anyway, I'm actually serious. Have you thought about what job you want to do when you finish school and move out? I would have thought you'd have it all planned by now."

Oh. Right. I guess I knew that on some level. *What do you want to be* really means what do you want to *do*. That's a good question. I don't think anyone has ever asked me that directly before, not even my mother. She has always seemed a lot more concerned with just getting me through one school so she can prepare me for the next one. She's never really talked about what's going to happen when we run out of schools for me. Maybe I should be a teacher so I can stay in school forever. Except I think there's an intelligence quotient requirement for teachers, and mine is too high.

"Not really." I don't think I should tell her about my movie-theater idea. I'm not sure wishing for something is the same as planning.

"I'm going into research. Molecular biology," Robert says, even though no one actually asked him directly.

"That's cool. I think." Angel looks at us both. She raises her eyebrows as if her face is trying to ask us a question.

"This is when you're supposed to ask me if I know what *I* want to do. Remember, that whole asking questions so we can have a conversation thing?" Angel pokes me on the arm, which hurts more than she thinks it does. I should never have told her about my social skills lessons. Now she's decided she's my private socialization tutor, which is rather ironic because I actually never see her socializing with anyone but me. And Robert, at least today, anyway. Why didn't she poke him? He forgot to ask her, too.

"Oh. I forgot. Do you know what you want to do when you grow up?"

"Why, *thank you* for asking," she answers in a tone that even I can tell is sarcastic. "Yes, I do. I want to be an actress. I want to be whoever I decide to be, and believe anything I want to believe without someone telling me different. I figure the best way to do that is to act. I was in the drama club at my last school, and I'm really good."

"Were you in any plays?" Robert asks the question, keeping the conversation alive, which is too bad because I'm getting rather tired of talking.

"Well, only one, and I didn't actually get to talk because I was just in the background of a crowd scene but I was still really good at looking natural, and I practice a lot in my room, and I know I'm good. I just have to decide what kind of actress I want to be and then go for it."

"Kind of actress?" He's still asking. Robert is definitely smarter in social skills than I am. Then again, if he wasn't here, I would have figured out a way to stop the whole conversation by now, which makes me wonder who the smartest one is after all.

"Yeah. There are two basic kinds of actresses. Fat and skinny. Fat actresses get lots of comedy roles and get to be the best friend, giving important advice a lot. Skinny actresses get to be funny sometimes, but they also get to be super dramatic and usually get the guy by the end of the movie. So I have to decide if I want to be the fat kind, since I'm already pretty much there, or get serious about my diet, so I can be the one who gets the guy."

She stops talking and looks at me expectantly, which I know is my cue to talk. But I'm not sure what to say. Every time Angel says the word *fat*, I get into trouble, and I still don't totally understand why. I know my mother told me never to ask a lady how much she weighs, not that I would anyway. Why would I care how much someone weighs, unless I have to lift them up? Since I can't imagine any scenario in which I would have to pick anyone up, I can't imagine ever wanting to know how much someone weighs. But I still don't understand why the word *fat* is so bad. It's nice and short, very descriptive. Efficient.

I look over at Robert, hoping he will decide it's his turn to talk again. He's smiling at me for some reason.

"Anyway, guys, I have to go get my books and head back up to the lab. Nice meeting you, Angel. See you later, Frederick. Good luck."

Good luck? Good luck with what?

"Bye, Robert. See you around." Angel gives him a little wave. I watch him walk out of the library and wish I could figure out a way to follow him.

"So, do you have an opinion?" Angel says before I can think of an escape route.

"No!" The word jumps out of me with more force than I expected, and she looks a little startled for a second. Then she grins at me and shrugs her shoulders.

"My mom thinks I should go on a diet now and get skinny. Not to get better acting parts but just to supposedly feel better about myself. What do you think?"

"I don't know if it would it make you feel better. I do know that everyone wants to be thin, which is strange because I am often teased by the Despisers for being thin." I shut my mouth tightly before any more words sneak out. I don't usually talk about my categories. They are no one's business but mine.

"The Despisers? Who're they?"

"Nobody. Just…no one."

"Yeah? Well, nobody and no one call me names, too."

"Just because you're fat?" I did it again. Words falling out of my mouth that didn't go through my filter. My mother and teachers worked so hard for so many years to make that filter. I really should try to use it more. I'm scared I've pissed her off again, but she just shakes her head at me and shrugs her shoulders.

"Fat. New. Glasses. Frizzy hair. Wrong clothes. Zits. Take your pick. But that's just school, right? School sucks, and pretty much everyone in it is full of crap. Except you. You're cool, you know?"

"No, I didn't know that. That isn't one of the names people usually call me."

She laughs. "Well, you are. So, do you like movies?"

"Yes." Movies used to be one of my favorite things.

"We should go to one together sometime."

"*Go* to one? At the theater? You and me together?" I've only ever gone to movies with my mother, and that one time with Robert. I don't know what it would be like to go to a theater with Angel. It would be a lot different from sitting in the Reject Room or hiding in the library with her. She'd probably talk the whole way through and get us kicked out.

"Yes, at the theater. Don't look so panicked. I'm not asking you out on a date. It's just two friends going to a movie. Platonic. I won't try to hold your hand. I won't even steal your popcorn. Movies are better in the theater. You can really get into them and just kind of forget about everything else. I like to imagine I'm up there on the screen with all the other actors, making lots of money and having everyone love me. So, do you want to go sometime?"

I should tell her that I sort of understand how she feels about movies—except for the money and having people love her part. I'm not much interested in money, and I definitely don't care if strangers love me or not. I should tell her that I used to dream about living inside of a movie in my very own theater. I should tell her that I'm surprised she wants me to go to a movie with her and that it sounds like it might be an interesting thing to do, even though it also seems a bit scary. And I definitely should tell her that she can't steal my popcorn because that would put germs on it, and then I couldn't eat it anymore.

"I'll ask my mother," I tell her.

"Sounds like a date!"

"*What?*"

"Just kidding." She grins.

"Don't waste your time with him. Fagface isn't into girls. You are a girl, right? Kind of hard to tell with all the flab."

It's Peter the Despiser again. I don't know how he found us in here. Despisers don't usually come into the library unless they're forced to by a teacher.

"Screw off jerkwad." Angel looks at him like he's the dirt that a worm crawls through.

"Oooh. Big and tough. I'm so scared."

"It doesn't look like you are in here to work, Mr. Murphy. Off you go!" Peter looks back at Mr. Nichols, the librarian, who has come up behind him. He usually sits at his desk at the front of the library, but I guess it finally got too loud over here.

"Sorry." Peter sounds more pissed than sorry but he leaves anyway, making sure he steps on my foot as he goes past. It hurts, but I don't say anything. Easier just to let him get out of here.

Apologies are strange things. Kids are taught to "say you're sorry" from the time we start talking as if somehow the words are magic and will fix whatever has been broken. I've had so many people say *sorry* to me that I can't even put a number on it, even though I have an extraordinary mind for numbers. It has never been my experience that hearing the word *sorry* makes any difference at all.

"It's Angel, right? Is everything all right? Was Peter bothering you?" Mr. Nichols looks at both of us.

"Oh, no. Everything's fine. Just getting some help with my homework," Angel says in a cheerful voice. Mr. Nichols nods, accepting her lie without seeming to notice that we don't look much like we're in here to work, either.

"Okay. I know how it can be in a new school. You let me know if you need anything."

"I will." Angel smiles as Mr. Nichols heads back to his desk.

"Why did you lie? He *was* bothering us." Although I'm not always that bothered by the things Peter says. A lot them just don't make any sense. Senseless things don't bother me much. Most of the time I just ignore them until they dissolve and float away.

"What's the point in telling the truth? What's the teacher going to do? Tell him to stop?"

"Yes."

"And after he stops right here and right now, what next?"

"He'll start again somewhere else." This I know from experience.

"So, why tell and make it worse? I can deal with it. We both can. Right?"

"Right."

She nods at me and I nod back.

I'm not sure if we were agreeing to the truth or a lie. I'm not sure it matters.

I'm not sure what matters anymore, except that she's gone and nothing is the way it was supposed to be, with so many lies and truths getting all tangled up together that I can't even tell the difference any more.

eight

My phone starts vibrating, telling me someone is trying to call. I look around my room, surprised for a second that I am at home. Seems to be a pattern today. I usually know where I am, but today has been confusing. I can't seem to keep track of my insides versus my outsides.

The phone rings again. Only three people have ever called me on my phone before.

I know it isn't Angel or my mother, so it has to be Robert. "Hello."

"Hey, what's going on? Everyone is talking about you."

I sit thinking for a few moments. I don't want to talk to Robert. I don't have anything to say to him.

"Come on. I know you're there. You answered the phone! Answer me. Come on."

What does that even mean? Come *on* what?

"Nothing." I say it quickly, hoping it sounds emphatic enough. I wish I was writing it instead, so I could use an exclamation point and then just end the conversation.

"It's something. You were at the cop shop. Is it about Angel? I heard she's missing."

"I answered some questions, that's all." That's mostly true.

"People are saying that you know where she is and won't tell. Or that you did something to her."

"What does *that* mean?"

"I don't know. That you made her run away or something."

"Why would I do that?" A better question would be *how* would I do that? She's bigger and tougher than I am.

"I don't know. I didn't say *I* thought that. Do you know where she is?"

"I can't talk about her."

"You can tell me. We're friends, aren't we?"

I don't know what being friends has to do with whether or not I can tell Robert anything, and I don't have Angel here to explain it to me. I'm getting more and more proof of what I always suspected. Friendship is highly overrated. Life is much less complicated if you stick with yourself. Quieter too. "I have to go now."

"What am I supposed to tell everyone?"

"Don't tell anyone anything. There's nothing to tell. Bye."

I end the call and shut off my phone for good measure, so there won't be any more calls. I shut off my computer also, so no one can message me there.

Robert's words are still written on the computer screen

inside of my mind though, and I'm having trouble shutting that one down.

People talking about me. People thinking I did something to Angel.

The Despisers are probably loving this. More reasons to hate me.

The Helpers probably hate me now, too.

The Avoiders are probably ignoring the whole thing.

I had this all under control. It was no one's business but ours. Everything organized and in its place, colors lined up in perfect order. Except now they're swirling out of control, crossing over each other and making everything the wrong color so that I don't know what I'm doing anymore.

I should never have answered the phone last week when she called me. That's when life really started to spin in the wrong direction.

"Kal? Hi, it's me. Angel."

"Oh, hi." I'm surprised to hear her voice. I never gave her my number. No one has my number except my mother and Robert. She must have read it off my phone. She's sneakier than I gave her credit for.

"You sound thrilled to hear from me. Can I come over to your house? I need to talk to you."

"To my house?" It's Sunday afternoon. My mother isn't home. She does grocery shopping on Sunday afternoons. She works during the week, and she says Saturdays are too busy at the stores so she always shops on Sundays when it's quieter. Sometimes I go with her, but I disagree about Sundays being quieter. There are lots of people at the store on Sundays. It's loud. Children cry and scream and things. Even worse, sometimes I see someone from school. No one says anything rude to me in front of my mother, but they give me looks that make me feel like they said something even if their mouths are closed. My mother never sees.

"Yes, to your house. Or somewhere else if that's a problem. I just need to talk to you."

"You're talking now." This is confusing. I see Angel at school and sometimes chat with her online. First she wants to go to a movie, and now she wants to come over to my house on a Sunday. She keeps changing the boundaries, making our friendship parameters bigger and bigger until they're overwhelming my life.

"Yeah, I know but this needs a face-to-face. Please?"

I guess she thinks that using the word *please* will make me think she is being polite and make me want to see her more.

"I don't know if my mother would like me to have someone here."

"Oh, is she strict about you having friends over?"

"I'm not sure. I don't really ever have friends over. Except Robert. And that was only twice."

"Oh. Okay. Well, is there somewhere else we can meet?"

"Behind my house. I have a place I go to that isn't my house."

"You mean in the woods back there? You live in front of, like, a forest don't you?"

"It's exactly a forest. I like to go there. No people."

"Well, I'll never find you in a forest. Can we meet in front of your house and then go to your spot? I really need to talk."

"I guess."

"Awesome. See you in ten."

No one has ever really *needed* to talk to me before. This sounds very serious. I hope she doesn't need me to talk back.

I go outside within ten minutes of her call, but she doesn't come for another five. Her face is all sweaty and her hair is frizzier than usual. Her eyes are red, and she is breathing heavily like she is having trouble finding air. This is probably because she ran, and she is fat. Fat people have trouble running. Their heavier bodies make it more difficult to move quickly. Oddly, I also have trouble running even though I am thin. This is because I never run unless I have to. I used to have to run more often when I was younger than I do now.

"Hi."

"Hi." I can't think of what to say next so I just turn and start walking. She follows me quietly. She's sniffing a bit, which I guess is because of her being out of shape. We live on the very edge of town. My mother always says she bought our house because it makes her feel like she's living in the country, even though she's still in the town. If you stand in our backyard, it does feel like you're far away. The forest behind us stretches for miles, right over to the next town, where it's probably in someone else's backyard. When I was small I wasn't allowed to cross over the back fence into the woods in case I got lost. Now I'm allowed but only as far as my spot.

"This is nice," Angel says as we stop walking. I wonder if

I should tell Angel my Treehenge joke. I think about it for a second and then decide against it. I have discovered that the only person who really likes my jokes is my mother, and I am beginning to suspect that her enjoyment is mostly an acting exercise.

I imagine that the trees must be very, very old to have figured out a way to actually grow through a giant rock like this. I like to come here and sit on the rock with my back against the trees. It's quiet and a good place for thinking. Angel's voice sounds unnaturally loud out here. I've never heard voices here before, except chipmunks' and birds'.

"Yes. I like it." I sit down against a tree. My own voice also sounds loud, and I feel like I've invaded the sanctity of the space somehow.

"It's quiet. Peaceful or whatever. Maybe I can just live here." She sits down and closes her eyes.

"Live here? You couldn't live here. This is a rock. And there are animals here. Deer and wolves and things." She opens her eyes and looks at me. She smiles, but it doesn't look right. It doesn't seem real somehow, as if she's imagining that she looks happy and has forgotten how to control her face.

"I know it's a rock. And I'm not afraid of Bambi, and I know for a fact that wolves don't attack humans because I did a project on them in grade four, and I got a C."

"A C?" What does her grade have to do with anything?

"Yeah, that's the grade you get when all the A's and B's are taken by guys like you. And even though I only get C's, I do know I can't live here. I just want to get away from this stupid school in this stupid town. I told my parents that we should move back to our old place and they just said that I'm old enough to understand that we had to move here for my dad's job."

"Why do you want to move back?"

"Why? Why do you think?"

"I don't know."

"I thought you, of all people, would know. I mean, it happens to you, too. It never stops. I just don't want to deal with it anymore. I mean there are some jerks in my old school too, but I had some friends there as well. It, I don't know, balanced better there, you know?"

"I don't think I do know."

She looks at me and shakes her head. She does that a lot when she's frustrated, usually with me. Right now she seems frustrated with the whole world.

"You really don't, do you? Nothing seems to really get to you, does it? I'm talking about the idiots at school who seem to think they're cool or whatever by making my life suck. I just can't take it anymore. Every day I have to listen to their crap about how fat or weird or ugly I am. I'm just sick of it."

Her voice sounds angry, but in a quiet way…the dangerous kind of anger that my mother sometimes has, but this isn't directed at me. I don't understand the way she's talking. She has never seemed very concerned about the things people at school do or say. She always says they're all full of crap.

"Do your parents know?" My mother has always told me I should tell her if someone bothers me at school. I used to tell her sometimes, but it usually didn't make them stop. It just made them bother me somewhere else. Kids still say stupid things to me, but mostly I don't let them bother me. That way, I don't have to tell anyone about it.

"I told them that it's worse here than at other schools I've been in. That's why I want to go home to Castleford. But they don't get it. They think I'll figure it out and settle in or some bullshit like that. They don't understand anything. All they think about is jobs and money and moving so that they can have better jobs and more money. If I could, I'd move back without them and live on my own."

"I don't think you're old enough to live without parents." Angel is not making any sense. She can't live alone. I can't imagine living without my mother. I mean, where would I go? Houses cost money. So do groceries and other essentials like the Internet.

"I know. I'm just wishing. Don't you ever just randomly wish for things you know you can't have?"

I look at her for a moment, considering her question. Somehow, I don't think she's talking about a movie theater. Although she does want to be an actress.

Logically speaking, I know it doesn't really make sense to want something you can't have. Most of the time I try to only want things that I know I *can* have.

"Not really. It's not very logical." She looks at me and laughs so quietly that it sounds more like a sigh.

"You're funny. You sound like a Vulcan. You make me feel better without even trying." Her words and face don't match. I think she's probably lying about feeling better, but I can never really tell when people aren't telling the truth.

"Oh." I say *oh* when I have absolutely no idea what I'm supposed to say. It's a useful syllable.

Am I supposed to be trying to make her feel better? I don't even understand why she's so upset. She seems...different today, like an angrier version of herself that I never met before. It's as if something has changed her.

Should I ask her about it?

"Yeah. Oh." She pretend smiles again and looks at her cell phone. "I gotta go. Thanks for listening. See you at school."

She runs off before I can say anything else. I didn't ask her. I suppose if she had something to tell me, she would have. She's never shy about talking.

No one ever thanked me for listening before. It's a lot easier to listen than to try and figure out what I'm supposed to be saying to people. My mother and my teachers and my workers have always been trying to get me to talk more. Social skills lessons. *How to Start a Conversation. How to Join a Conversation. How to Interrupt a Conversation.*

I'd like conversations more if all I had to do was listen.

Angel doesn't even need me to talk for us to have a conversation, even though she's been trying to teach me how to do it properly ever since I met her. She does most of the talking. I'd be happy to let her do all of it.

I wonder who she's talking to now?

I wonder if she knows that someone's trying to get *me* to talk now?

I wonder if she knows that I remember what she told me.
That I should say it inside my head like a mantra every time
I'm afraid I might accidentally open my mouth.

Don't tell
Don't tell
Don't tell.

nine

"So, I've got some good news and some bad news. Which one do you want first?"

"I don't know." It's the Tuesday after her phone call and we're sitting on my Treehenge rock, where I'm trying to eat my after-school snack. Angel basically followed me home from school like a lost puppy, and now she's eyeing my apple.

"You don't know or you're not interested? Are you going to finish that?" Angel points to half of my apple. I always cut my fruit in half so that I can see what I'm eating. I pick it up and hand it to her. She already took a bite out of it when she first sat down. She didn't ask me if she could, she just did it. If she had asked me I would have said no. I read an article once that estimated that we swallow a hundred billion microbes of oral bacteria every twenty-four hours, and I bet a lot of those are the unhealthy kind. I have more than enough of my own germs without Angel adding some of hers. Lots of people say that a dog's mouth is cleaner than a person's, which would mean I'd be better off if Angel actually *was* a puppy. I don't really believe that, though. Germs are germs, and I don't eat anything that's been drooled on by any mouth but mine.

"You can have it," I offer generously.

"Thanks. This is good. My mom always says I don't eat enough fruit so this would make her happy."

"Is that the good news?"

"Ha! You made a joke! I'm obviously having a good effect on you."

She punches me on the shoulder with her sharp knuckles. She does that fairly often, mostly when she seems happy with something I've said. She often tells me I made a joke when I wasn't even trying to. Apparently I am a much funnier person than I thought. I can't figure this punching thing out, though. Angel doesn't seem to have rules that govern physical assault.

"No, that isn't the good news. The good news is that I've figured out a solution to my problem. The bad news for you is that I really need to tell someone about it, and the only person I know who'll listen is you. Everyone else around here basically hates me."

"Just the Despisers." I said it again. I didn't mean to do that!

"The *what*?" She grins, a real one, the kind that teases without hurting. She's definitely much happier today, more like the original version of herself that I'm used to.

"Nothing." Nothing is what you say when you have said

something, but you regret saying it, and you are hoping the other person didn't actually hear you. I didn't mean to say the word *Despisers* out loud again. My categories are no one's business but mine.

"No, not nothing. Come on, what did you say? You can tell *me*."

No not nothing. Is that a triple negative?

"It's just what I call them. Despisers."

"Despisers. Right. Because they hate you. I have other words for them. You want to hear?"

"Not really. And I don't know if they hate me or not. It just seemed like the right word for the way they act. Something like that." It's hard to explain it to her out loud. The word is supposed to be safe inside my head where it doesn't need to be explained to anyone but me. I don't think the Despisers really hate me. I don't think they have any emotions toward me in particular. I think they just use hateful words against people because it's what they do. I've never really thought about why. I try not to care much. They can't hurt me if I don't care.

"It's a good word. So, anyway, the good news is I figured out how to get away from the *Despisers*. And everyone else in this hole-in-the-world, dead-end, creep-filled town."

"Oh."

"Yeah, *oh*. Don't sound so excited for me. I might think you care or something. Anyhow, the point is, I'm going home. Back to my old place."

"Your parents are moving back?"

"No, just me." She smiles as she shakes her head and

crosses her arms. She leans back against a tree and looks up at the leaves. "I do like it here. It's the nicest part of this town."

"You're moving back alone? How will you live?" We already talked about this. Why are we having two conversations about the same thing?

"Not actually alone. Well, I'm going there alone, but I won't be alone when I get there. I have a plan. A semi-secret plan."

This is the point where I should have stopped listening. I should have told her I didn't want to know her plan.

"I'm going to tell you about it, but you can't tell anyone else, okay? Not until everything is settled. Okay?"

"Okay." Two syllables signifying nothing. And everything.

"I have a friend back home. Celina. We hung out together at school with a couple of other kids. No one bugged us much when we were together, so we just stayed together, you know?"

I shrug my shoulders. Another useful gesture that means whatever the person looking at you decides it means.

"Safety in numbers or whatever. Anyway, I've been talking to her and telling her how lame it is around here, and she agrees that I should come back. She said I could come and stay at her place until my parents see the light."

"See the light?"

"Yeah. See that I'm serious about not staying here. That they can move back and have me with them, or they can stay here and see me on weekends and holidays. Like a divorce. Except I'm divorcing my parents."

It doesn't sound like a very good plan to me. I don't know

why she thinks she has to leave just because some kids are bugging her. It's what they do. Leaving won't change it. It will just make it happen somewhere else. I thought she knew that. Besides, I don't think she can divorce her parents. She can't just move away and live somewhere else. I think that her parents can go and get her and make her come back.

I don't say anything, though. It's really none of my business.

"So, I'm leaving Friday. I've saved the money up for bus fare. Birthday and Christmas cash from my granny. I bought the ticket already."

"Do your parents know yet?" I don't think my mother would be too happy if I bought a ticket for a bus that was going to take me away from her.

"No! Of course, not. Once I get there, I'll let them sweat for a while and then I'll call them. I'll wait just long enough for them to get worried, but not long enough to get the cops or anyone else involved. They'll be in a big panic and just starting to freak out, and I'll call them and explain the way things are. They'll be totally happy I'm not dead in a ditch and totally freaked that I left on my own. It's a perfect plan. Practically foolproof. Everyone wins, and no one gets hurt."

"And they'll let you stay?"

"They'll know how serious I am."

"Your friend's parents will let you stay?"

"She said so. At least until my parents figure it out."

"Oh."

"We can keep in touch. I'll keep you posted. I think you'd

like my other school. Fewer Despisers there."

My word sounds odd coming out of her mouth. Wish I hadn't told her. It isn't mine anymore.

"I'm fine here."

"Seriously? I've watched them go after you. They never leave you alone. All the gay crap. Are you, by the way?"

"What?"

"Gay."

"I don't know."

"You don't know if you like guys or girls? Shouldn't you know that by sixteen?"

"I'm not sure when you're supposed to know. I don't think about it all that much."

"You don't think about being gay or sex in general?"

I think we already had this talk also. Angel likes to revisit things. It gets me confused. I'm already confused enough by the way she's acting. "Both."

"So, you've never had a crush on anyone. Wanted to kiss anyone or anything?"

"No."

"Guess you're a late bloomer then. That's what my mom says I am. Except she's not talking about sex when she says it. She means my looks. She pretends it doesn't matter to her that I'm not all pretty and thin, but then she says stuff like that. Like I'm an ugly bud on some crappy tree that might turn into a beautiful flower someday. Because I'm not one now. My mother is. All skinny and beautiful. I think it bothers her that I turned out like this."

"I don't think you're ugly."

"But you do think I'm fat!"

"I didn't say anything about fat!" *This* time. How did I manage to say the wrong thing when I didn't even say the word? Sometimes it's better not to talk. Most times.

Angel looks at me with angry eyes for a split second and then switches personalities again. Split second. Like splitting an atom. Splitting an Angel—as if there's some kind of remote attitude control that keeps changing her channel without telling me first.

"It was implied. Oh, don't look so scared, Kal. I'm not really mad. It's cool. I know you like me. As a friend, I mean. You're my only friend around here. That's why I had to share the good news with you. And only you."

She said she had good news and bad news. But it was all the same news.

It was only bad.

She said it was perfect.

She said no one would get hurt.

She said I had to keep it to myself because she's my friend.

She made me swear.

Don't tell

Don't tell

Don't tell.

ten

LOCAL TEEN MISSING
Fifteen-year-old Angel Martinez has been officially declared missing from her home in the town of Topego. According to local police, Angel was last seen leaving school on Friday afternoon. Search parties comprised of local law officials and volunteers have been scouring the town and nearby communities with no success. Police have issued an Amber alert in the case. Anyone with any information regarding Angel's whereabouts is asked to call the TIPS line at 1-800-555-6719.

The Sunday morning headline yells at me. A picture of Angel frowning at the camera sits beside it. It's not a very good picture of her. She would say it makes her look fat. She says everything makes her look fat. Which is pretty much true.

I did it again! If I said something like that out loud in front her, she'd probably punch me for real, the angry kind that tries to hurt, and then I'd probably have a permanent bruise on my arm, like a tattoo to remind me that I should stop using that word even inside my head. Angel told me that it's an insult, even though I think it's just descriptive. Besides, I just don't think there's anything wrong with being fat. Or thin. Or tall. Or short. Or white. Or black. Or anything else that makes you who you are.

Fat. It's just a word. But I am going to stop using it anyway.

I wish Angel was here. I'd gladly let her tattoo my arm if it would just make her come home and end this mess we're both in. I wish I understood why she left.

I can't let myself think about it. I can't think about the fact that she went away and that I knew about it.

I can't even let my mind tell, or my mouth might accidentally join in.

It wasn't supposed to be like this. It's too long. She said twelve hours when she ambushed me on the way home from school Thursday night to talk about her plan again.

"I figure twelve hours, fifteen at the most, and then I'll call my parents. Let them worry overnight. No one else is going to get too excited until I've been gone a lot longer than that. I'm pretty sure you can't even call the cops until after twenty-four hours."

"Pretty sure? Didn't you research it?"

"Sure enough. And no, I didn't research it. At least not officially. But I watch a lot of cop shows on TV. The reality kind, not the fake stuff. I know how it works. Mostly."

Pretty sure. Mostly. I don't like those odds. I like to be completely sure and know exactly how things work.

"Maybe I should look it all up for you first. Just to make sure."

"Thanks, but no thanks. I'm doing it this way. It's all decided. I have everything in place. All you have to do is nothing."

"Right." How do you do nothing? It's impossible. You're always doing something. If you're doing nothing, you shouldn't be using the verb *doing* because it implies that *something* is happening. Not *nothing*. Double negative. Hate those.

"Seriously, Kal. I took a big risk telling you at all. But I had to tell someone. You know?"

"Okay." I don't know at all. I don't know why she had to tell me anything. It's her business, not mine. But I don't feel guilty saying *okay* when it isn't because, after all, *okay* doesn't actually mean anything. At least not to me. It's just a couple of syllables that mean something to other people.

"You're saying it's okay, but I can tell you don't get it. You're not as hard to read as you think."

"The only thing I don't get is why you told me something that isn't supposed to be told."

She looks at me in that way she has that means she can't decide whether to laugh or punch me in the arm. "I told you because I thought that you would be the only person who might notice I'm gone. I thought you might wonder where I went. Or even, like, worry or something touchy-feely like that. You know, have an emotion or something." She's not smiling. She wants to punch me I think.

I have emotions. Lots of them. Everyone does. Most people wear them on their faces and in their voices for the whole world to see and hear. I think emotions are private and should be worn on the inside where they're safe.

"Oh. I didn't think of that."

"Well, think about it now. Would you wonder or worry or any other W words if I suddenly disappeared without telling you first?"

Would I wonder or worry if I came to school, and Angel wasn't sitting in the Reject Room at lunch time, ready to fill my ears with words that I only half listen to? Up until a few weeks ago, I didn't even know there was an Angel. If she wasn't there anymore would I feel different?

She isn't going to be there anymore. I'm going to be eating alone again. Quietly. I hadn't thought of that before. No one will smile at me and tell me I'm funny, even when I'm not trying to be. No one will talk to me except Robert, sometimes, and Peter Murphy the rest of the time.

No one will ask me to the movies, even though we never actually went.

I was scared at the idea of going to the movie with her, and now I don't have to do it. I guess I should feel relieved. But I'm not sure that's what I'm feeling.

I have to think about it some more. Angel says you aren't supposed to think about your feelings. You're just supposed to let them happen. Thinking and feeling are two different things. I have to think about that, too. I have never really separated them in my mind. I think about everything. Thinking is the way you sort things out so that everything is in its correct place and your colors are all where they are meant to be, so that they don't swirl in a random pattern that makes everything confused.

"Could you think a little faster? I have things to do." She punches me on the arm. I knew it.

"Sorry." She should be the one saying sorry. That hurt.

"I'm not looking for sorry. I just wondered if you were going to miss me or not. Man, Kal, it's like pulling teeth."

"Pulling teeth?" I hope that isn't the next step up from the punch on the arm.

"Just a stupid expression my mother uses. It just means it's impossible to get an answer out of you."

"Oh. Well, that's because I don't have an answer right now. And I do have teeth that technically could be pulled. So the expression doesn't apply. My mother always says it's like getting blood from a stone. Stones don't have blood, so that fits better." Angel looks at me. It's still her punch-on-the-arm expression. I hope it stays an expression. I think I'm starting to bruise.

"Okay. I think we're done. I'm going to say good-bye to you now, instead of tomorrow in school. If this all works out, and I don't come back, I will miss you whether you miss me or not. You are definitely different from any other friend I've had." She shocks me by changing the rules and ruffling my hair. It doesn't hurt, but it feels strange and I reach up to pat the hairs back into place. This time Angel does laugh.

"You're quite a guy, Kal. I hope you find someone else to hang out with. You shouldn't keep all that to yourself. Take care. I'll be in touch after everything settles down."

"All right. Bye." She looks at me and shakes her head.

"Slow down a bit, I'm not done yet! Thanks for this, Kal. I knew you'd help me out. You're a good friend, you know?"

"No, I didn't know that." She laughs for a second. Her eyes are shiny and red, and she sniffs and wipes at them a bit.

"No, I guess you didn't. Well you are. Oh, and because you are such a good friend, I need you to remember one thing, or the whole plan goes down the toilet."

"What?"

"Don't tell. Anyone, anything. Okay? Seriously. Don't tell. Not even your mom."

"Okay."

"No, not just okay. I need you to swear."

"Swear?"

"Like an oath kind of swearing. Here take my hand." She grabs my hand before I can stop her. I don't like to touch people, but she doesn't give me a choice. Her hand feels wet and I can imagine germs squiggling around our two palms, leaving hers and moving onto mine. It makes me feel a little sick.

"Repeat after me. I will not tell anyone about Angel Martinez's whereabouts."

"I will not tell anyone about Angel Martinez's whereabouts."

"We'll shake on it three times, and each time you say 'Don't tell' so that it gets stuck in your brain." It's a silly idea and not much of an oath, but I want to get rid of her hand so I nod and shake.

"Don't tell." First shake. I can feel the germs creeping onto my skin.

"Don't tell." Second shake. They're starting to dance on my palm.

"Don't tell." Last one. I break contact quickly and put my hand behind my back, trying to wipe it on my pants without Angel noticing. She looks at me and raises her eyebrows, shaking her head.

"Okay. I guess this is it. I'll let you go find some hand sanitizer. Bye, Kal. See ya around."

"Well, not really. You probably won't be around here anymore after tomorrow."

"It's just an expression, Kal."

"Oh." Not a very logical one.

"Kal?"

"Yes?"

"Can I have a hug good-bye? It's what friends do when they aren't going to see each other anymore."

My body instantly recoils at the question. It was hard enough to shake her hand, and I really want to follow her suggestion and find my hand sanitizer right now. My scalp is still tingling from her assault on my follicles and I am itching to get home and wash it. A hug means full body contact.

But she played the friend card again. She uses that one all the time. We agreed that she's the expert on friends and that I'm the student. I'm not supposed to question her so-called wisdom. That was a bad agreement on my part. But I don't break agreements. It's my personal code.

We're both fully clothed so there won't be any skin to skin. If I change right away, it should be all right. My mother hugs me sometimes when I can't get away from her. I survive those. I can survive this.

"All right." Even though it's not.

"Great. Here we go." She steps forward with both arms out, reaching for me. I accidentally step backwards but she keeps coming toward me. Before I have a chance to change my mind, she grabs my shoulders and pulls me against her, wrapping her arms across my back. It feels tight and uncomfortable, like being trapped in the car, and I'm not sure I can breathe. I'm afraid to move. My arms are down at my sides, not sure what their job is. I should be telling them they're supposed to hug her back because that's what my mother taught me.

It goes on for a long time. Seconds. Minutes. Hours. I can't tell. It's too warm with all this body heat. I can smell Angel's shampoo. Her frizzy hair is tickling my nose, but I don't feel like laughing. I can smell other odors, too, but I don't want to think about that.

"I'm not letting go until you hug me back." Her voice is muffled by my shoulder. Now there are germs from her mouth slipping into the fabric of my sweater. They're going to get in there and worm their way through onto my skin and into my body. I have to do something.

I tell my arms to reach up and circle her back. I keep my bare hands from making contact by crossing my wrists. Luckily I have long arms. Unusual on such a short body. Gives the Despisers a whole category of ape-related adjectives to use when they run out of ways to call me small, stupid, or gay.

I hold her for just a second and then drop my arms. It's her turn now. I held up my end. Literally.

She holds on for another infinite second and then sighs and drops her arms. Before I see it coming, she reaches up with her face and kisses me on the cheek. I wince before I can stop my face from doing it. My mother always told me that I shouldn't make a face when someone kisses me, especially her. She said it hurts the kisser's feelings. But what about my feelings? Does the kisser worry about how I feel having someone's saliva planted on my skin? Ever heard of mononucleosis? They call it the kissing disease for a reason.

"I'll miss you, Kal." She wipes a tear from her eye. I don't know why the tear is there. This is what she wants, and she's getting it. She should be glad.

"I think I might miss you too," I say back. This is true. I think it is going to feel different at school without Angel there. Different in a not-so-great way. I have a strange feeling inside, an empty sensation like I'm hungry, but I'm not thinking about food. I might be starting to miss her already. I guess I'll know in a few days for sure. After she's really gone.

I saw her one more time on Friday at lunchtime in the Reject Room. We did talk to each other but not about her plan. We just pretended it was a normal day. I think Angel talked about some TV show she watched the night before, and I pretended to be interested.

When the bell rang, she just walked out of the room like it was any other day. We didn't even say good-bye again.

And now she's just gone.

She's been gone for more than forty hours, and there's been no phone call to her parents.

Twelve hours after she left, I was in the police station being questioned about her. Her mom and dad noticed right away and pushed every possible panic button. She should have researched it. *I* should have researched it.

Forty hours, and she hasn't called her parents yet.

Forty hours, and she hasn't called me.

Forty hours, and she isn't where she's supposed to be, or she would have done what she said she was going to do.

It was supposed to be over by now. No one was supposed to be out searching for her.

I don't know where she is.

Now I don't have to lie anymore.

For a second I can feel the warm and kind of slimy feeling of touching her hand again. I sit perfectly still, looking at my palm, wondering if it still has Angel germs living there with mine. I can still hear our words, whispering at me through the leaves, shifting as the wind tries to push them off the trees.

Don't tell

Don't tell

Don't tell.

Useless words because now I don't have anything to tell.

eleven

"In local news, grade ten student Angel Martinez is still missing. No one has heard from her since she left school on Friday. Police and local volunteers continue to coordinate search efforts in the surrounding area."

I've been checking the TV newscasts for updates all morning and now they've added a video to Angel's story. The announcer disappears and is replaced by another woman with red-rimmed and watery-looking eyes. Her nose looks sore, like she's been blowing it too much. She has glasses on, but she takes them off to wipe her eyes. I wonder who she is and why I am looking at her.

"Please help us find our daughter. If anyone knows where she is, please tell us. Or even if you have an idea of where we can look. If someone out there has my baby, please give her back to me. Angel, if you can hear me, I want you home. I love you."

Her watery eyes spill over into a waterfall down her face as the picture fades back to the announcer.

"Anyone with any information at all that could help with this search, please call the number on the bottom of the screen. The police have indicated that time is of the essence, so please, call now if you have even the slightest idea of where she could be."

The lady with the waterfall is Angel's mother. She looks much sadder than Angel expected her to be.

Angel didn't call her. Which definitely means her plan didn't work.

I have to do something. What am I supposed to do?

She told me not to tell. She said that friends don't tell on friends.

The police and the news announcer and my mother say I have to tell what I know, which isn't much. But it could be something.

She was going to the city to find her friend. She was going to stay there until her parents came.

If Angel's safe at her friend's house, why didn't she call her mother?

If I tell what I know, how much trouble will I be in? If I don't tell what I know, how much trouble will Angel be in?

I don't what the rule is. Who can tell me? If I ask my mother, she will know that I know something, and I will end up telling anyway.

I can't ask Robert. He likely wouldn't know. He doesn't know all the friendship rules. The boss of the friendship rule book is Angel. She's the one who knows all the rules.

And she isn't answering her phone.

I've been thinking about it all morning.

There's only one thing I can do. I have to go and find her myself. She'll tell me what to do.

"Frederick? It's lunch time. I've called you twice already. Where are you?" My mother's voice gets sharper every day, slicing with every edge. She's worried I think. Or angry. I can't always tell them apart. I don't think she can either.

"I'll be right there!" I call back to her with a cheerful sound that I paint onto my voice. I'm trying to fool her with pleasantness.

I grab my knapsack and take out my homework. I stash it under my bed and pull out my comic box. Inside is an envelope that my mother doesn't know about. It has money in it. Sometimes I sell things on eBay, like first edition Archie comics still in the wrapper that my grandmother bought me, thinking she was doing something wonderful. I'm not sure why I don't tell my mother about it, but I suspect that she wouldn't like it.

I push the envelope to the bottom of my bag for safety and cram some clothes on top. They will be wrinkled when I try to put them on, which will not feel particularly nice, but I don't know how long this will take and wrinkled clothes are likely better than dirty ones.

I look at my room. I hope that this doesn't take more than a day. I don't much like sleeping anywhere that isn't my room. My room is safe. Other rooms are not. Especially hotel rooms. They have bacteria growing on every surface, sneaky little guys who hide in plain sight just waiting for someone to come close enough to give them a new home. My mother tried to take me to a hotel once, but it took so long to clean it that we didn't have much time for sightseeing, so we don't really travel much.

I don't want to go on a bus and drive to another place. But I think I have to.

I know what city her friend lives in. I don't know the actual address, but I can probably figure all of that out when I get there.

My tablet slips unsuspectingly into its case totally unaware that it's heading off on a journey. Now all I have to do is figure out a way to get away without my mother wondering where I am.

"Sorry I took so long. I was just talking to Robert. He was wondering if I could stay at his house tonight. We have a project due, and he thought we could work on it." The lie oozes out of me, leaving a gross guilty taste behind in my mouth.

My mother smiles at me. She seems pleased. I feel grosser.

"Well, I wouldn't usually say yes seeing as you have school in the morning, but since it's for homework, I guess it's all right. It might help take your mind off your other friend for a bit. Are you sure you're up for this?" she says, totally unaware of what she is really asking me. She's asking if I think I can handle sleeping at someone else's house, which is a valid question, considering my less than stellar history with sleepovers of any kind, even at my grandmother's house.

"I'm not sure, but I want to try."

"That's great. I'm sure you'll be fine. If you're not, just call me. I'll still be proud of you for trying." She smiles kindly. I am totally grossed out by myself.

"Thanks, Mom. I think I'll head over there now."

"What about your pajamas and toothbrush and clean clothes?"

"Oh, I already packed them, just in case you said yes." I lied again! Without even thinking about it! I'm getting too good at this. Mom's radar seems to be malfunctioning because she believes me again.

"All right then. Have a nice time, and I'll see you tomorrow after school."

"Okay. Bye."

I move quickly so that I don't change my mind.

I head off down the street toward Robert's place. When I'm sure I'm out of sight of the house, I take a wrong turn and walk toward the bus station. Well, it's not really a bus station. Our town is pretty small for a bus station. It's really a store down on Mill Street that sells tickets for buses to about three or four cities.

I know that there's a bus this afternoon. There's a bus to the city every morning at nine-thirty and every afternoon at one-thirty, seven days a week. I know this because Angel told me when she made the mistake of telling me her plan.

I didn't want to know her plan. Why did she tell me? And then why did she tell me not to tell? Now my life is upside down and I'm trying to walk around with my feet in the air.

"I'd like one ticket for the one-thirty bus to Castleford, please."

The clerk looks me up and down for a second. I panic for a moment, wondering if there's some age restriction for buying tickets. But there can't be, or Angel wouldn't be gone.

"One-way or round trip?"

"Oh. Round trip, I guess." I dig down to the bottom of my bag and pull out my envelope.

"That's twenty-five dollars. You have a student card?"

I have to lie. I do have a student card, but I can't show it to him. I don't want him to know who I am.

"Not on me. I think I lost it." Adding "I think" makes it less of a lie. At least, I think it does.

"Well, that's okay for today. You're obviously under twenty. I'll let it go this time."

I hand him the money and he hands me a ticket. It all seems so easy. He doesn't even ask me why I'm going.

"Bus'll be here in fifteen minutes. Have a good trip." His eyes are looking toward me but they aren't looking at me. He seems to have eye shields like mine. Probably important to have them when you have to deal with so many people every day. I can't imagine being in a job where you have to talk to people you don't even know every day. Or people you do know, for that matter.

I've never been on a bus that isn't a school bus before. I am not looking forward to it. I didn't like the school bus. Locked inside a moving trap with lots of loud kids throwing word darts at me, trying to get them to stick into me and hurt. There are no teachers on a school bus to tell the Despisers to stop.

I don't think that the people on this bus will be loud, but I will still be trapped.

Maybe I shouldn't be doing this. Maybe I should just tell

my mother everything, which isn't really very much, and she'll take care of everything, which could be a lot.

She'll tell the police about Angel's plan, and the police will tell her parents. *They* can go and look for her instead of me.

If I tell, I won't have to deal with it.

If I tell, someone else will go and find Angel.

If I tell, Angel will never speak to me again. I know this because she told me.

She told me not to tell.

She said it over and over. She said we're friends, and friends don't tell on friends.

"Are you getting on?"

The bus driver is staring at me. Right at me without any shields. I put mine up quickly. I'm going to need all the protection I can get.

The bus smells. Diesel fuel. It's snorting at me, puffing smoke in my face, a dragon waiting to swallow me, to hold me hostage deep inside until it spews me out, partially digested and screaming for mercy.

"I said, are you getting on?" His voice is louder now. I've probably made him angry. I don't like angry people.

His question is a good one. Wish I had a good answer. I don't know what to do. I'm hugging my knapsack like it's my best friend—except that I don't usually hug my friends. Actually I have never hugged anyone except my mother. And Angel, who made me hug her. Who kissed me.

Who's lost somewhere and might need to be found.

"Yes." I keep my shields up and move quickly up the stairs

before my stupid mind can change itself. I try to get by the driver without contact.

"Ticket please." His voice stops me. His hand is held out toward me. I look down at my own hand, which is clutching the ticket so tightly it's all wrinkled. Maybe it won't work all wrinkled, and I'll be kicked off the bus and won't have to go.

"Okay. Find yourself a seat. I think there's one or two at the back." He takes his eyes off me and puts them on the road. I look down at the rows of seats. They all seem to be holding people, who all seem to be looking at me.

I turn up my shield power to full and start to make my feet move down the aisle. I don't want to look at anyone, but I don't have a choice. I have to look so that I can find an empty seat. Why are so many people traveling to Castleford, anyway?

"There's room here." A voice to my left stops my feet. A lady, who looks like she might be the same age as my mother, is smiling up at me and patting the seat beside her. The bus is still standing still, and it occurs to me that everyone here is likely waiting for me to sit down so that the bus driver can start the bus. That's the way it always was on the school bus. Everyone would yell at me to hurry up and sit down.

I don't want all of these people to start yelling. I look at the lady. I don't smile back because I can't think of a reason that I would want to smile at a stranger on a bus. But I do sit down.

"You can put your bag up top, if you like," she says. I am still hugging my knapsack to my chest. It makes me feel just a tiny bit safer, like I have a piece of home attached to me.

I shake my head and grab the bag more tightly. I don't

look at her just in case I have made her angry by not listening.

"That's all right then. You seem a bit nervous. Haven't traveled alone before?"

I can't tell if it's a question or a statement. Her voice went up at the end, but the words don't seem right. Some are missing. I don't know if she expects me to answer her or not. When I'm nervous, I forget all of the rules, even the ones I usually know.

"So, why are you heading into the city on a Sunday? Are you visiting family?"

Those are definitely questions and I know that the rule is you answer questions politely especially when someone as old as your mother asks them. Except you don't have to talk to strangers. I don't know the rule about strangers on a bus that you're going to be trapped with while heading to a city you don't know to find a person who might not want to be found.

I shake my head. I can't answer her questions no matter what the rule book says.

I'm on the bus. I've made my decision.

I can't tell.

twelve

The air inside of a dragon is hot and stale. It doesn't circulate properly, and there isn't enough for everyone to have their fair share. The acrid fumes from leftover fire breath swirl around my head, trying to get inside of my nose and mouth so that they can burn me from the inside out. I'm afraid to breathe them in, so I try to hold my breath. But I can't hold my breath forever. I can't even hold it for minutes. I try burying my face in my bag, hoping the essence of home can cancel out the essence of dragon.

"Are you all right?" The lady's voice interrupts my search for home and I accidentally breathe in the foul air. It rushes inside of me and grabs my lungs, squeezing them until I can't find the strength to send it back out.

"It's all right. Just relax. Here, try breathing into this." I try not to listen to her because it's her fault I can't breathe in the first place, but she's shoving a bag into my face. It smells sweet.

"It's a good thing I brought my donut onto the bus. I don't tend to travel with a paper bag most of the time but I just had a craving for something sweet today. Here you go, just breathe deeply into this, and you'll feel a better in a jiffy."

I don't know what a jiffy is, and I don't want to breathe into a donut bag that has been touched by who knows how many people, but I also don't want to die inside this dragon. She's got the bag plastered against my face and I don't really have a choice. I let the air out into the bag.

"Just breathe in and out slowly a few times."

Breathe back in? The air in the bag just came from trying to kill me. If I breathe it back in, I'll die.

I push the bag away and shake it so that the bad air will leave. I'm still holding my breath. I need to suck more air in, but I don't know where to find it.

"Here, it's all right. Try again." Her voice is kind. Like a Helper, only real. I take the bag, hoping that all the bad air really left it, and hold it back over my mouth. I breathe slowly in and out like she said. The bag crackles, moving with my air. My stomach grumbles, confused by the sweet smell of donut sugar.

"My son used to have panic attacks on air planes. Claustrophobic. Thought the air was going to kill him. It took him years to realize that it wouldn't. Always carried a paper bag with him. The other thing that helped was the little air vent. These buses have them too. They're better than the ones on planes because they're actually bringing in air from the outside. Here we go."

I suddenly feel a stream of cool air on the top of my head. I slowly move my head back away from the bag and look up. There's a little round knob above my head, with a tiny air hole that is letting in a stream of air that seems to be aiming right at me. I breathe it in, and it feels clean and almost safe.

My lungs stop hurting. The dragon's nefarious plan to kill me has been foiled.

"You look better now. Not quite so green."

I touch my face. Green? Maybe the dragon wasn't trying to eat me. Maybe it was trying to assimilate me.

"You just try to relax. We'll be there in no time."

She turns her attention away from me and into a book. I'm glad she brought a book. I wish I had thought of that. I like books. I can walk into them and stay there for a while. I can live inside the words and no one will bother me. I know I can find a book on my tablet, but I like reading from actual paper pages better. My mother says I'm a throwback.

I look at my watch. No time. How can we be there in no time? Everything takes *some* time. According to my calculations, I've been trapped on here for at least thirty minutes so we'll be there in about an hour's worth of time. Sixty minutes. Thirty-six hundred seconds. More or less.

Hopefully less.

I know that it's an illusion, but time does seem to move at different speeds depending on what you're doing. When I'm playing on my computer or walking in my woods, time goes so fast I feel like it's racing against me and always winning. I've never been a very good runner. I've always hated gym class because I'm terribly non-athletic, and the jocks (not one of my categories but the word they call themselves), tend to make fun of the non-athletes. I especially don't like the change room because the teacher never comes in there, on account of the need for privacy. But it makes me wonder about the need for safety. No one is safe from the Despisers when you're in the change room.

I try to get into a bathroom stall before a Despiser catches me and blocks the way. Sometimes, if I can't get behind a locked door to change, I don't change at all, and I just tell the gym teacher I forgot my clothes at home. Then the gym teacher gets mad, and the Despisers all laugh. Them laughing in front of the teacher is better than what happens alone in the change room.

Why am I thinking about the change room? Where was my head trying to go? Oh, right. Time. Moving at different speeds depending on what you're doing. When I'm in the change room, and I can't get out, Time doesn't move at all. It just freezes, laughing at me along with the Despisers.

Lots of Despisers are also Jocks. Multitasking.

Sitting inside a dragon's belly—with a kind but interfering lady, who reminds me of my mother (who is also frequently kind and often interfering)—and waiting for it to spew me out with all of the other undigested bits of dragon feed masquerading as people is going to slow Time down to a crawl. If we were racing today, I would win. But we're not racing today. Time is staying behind me, just out of sight, so that I can't figure out when I'm going to get out of this place.

The tiny stream of air is keeping me from jumping out

of the window. I want to thank the lady, but I'm afraid that talking will take up too much air. I might swallow it again. I'm not sure the mini airstream is enough to support my voice and keep my lungs from being poisoned.

Time also moves slowly when you have to pee, and you can't get to a bathroom. Your bladder starts to hurt, and all you can think about is what it's going to feel like to get into a bathroom and empty it out. Robert says his back teeth are floating when he has to go really badly. I don't really like that expression much. If your back teeth are floating when you have to go to the bathroom, it would imply that something besides saliva is in your mouth. Yuck.

I have to pee now, but I can't. There is a bathroom at the back of the bus, but I know it will be very, very small. One very, very small bathroom for all of these not-so-very-small people isn't what I call good sanitation. Public bathrooms are one of the places germs like to spend a great deal of their time.

So I have to wait. Fifty-five more minutes. Thirty-three hundred seconds.

I have to stop thinking about pee.

Now I'm thinking about my back teeth floating.

Maybe if I close my eyes and pretend to be asleep, I can fool Time into moving faster. Time really goes quickly when you're asleep. Your body can forget that it has to go to the bathroom if you get deep enough into your dreams. Or course, then you dream about oceans and taps dripping, and sometimes you pee in the bed, and then your mother shakes her head at you, and you feel like a loser because you wake up drowning in your own urine because you're a big baby who can't control his bladder, even though you're ten years old and…

Now I'm not ten years old, and I don't dream about dripping taps anymore, and I'm *not* going to wet this bus seat.

Just to be safe, I'll stay awake. It's not much longer now. I'll just close my eyes so that the nice bag lady beside me won't talk to me, or stick any more of her garbage in my face.

That wasn't a very nice thought. My mother wouldn't be impressed with me if she knew I'd had it.

I'll try another one. I'll just close my eyes so that the nice lady, who reminds me of my mother, won't ask me any more questions about where I'm going, or why. I don't want to accidentally say anything that I shouldn't.

I don't even know if it's the right thing anymore. I just know it's what Angel told me to keep in my mind. I'm good at keeping things in my mind and saying them to myself over and over and over. Saying and doing things over and over and over makes them safe.

At least it used to.

I'm not so sure anymore.

Don't tell

Don't tell

Don't tell.

No, it doesn't feel safe at all.

thirteen

"We're here, dear. Do you have someone meeting you at the station?"

Her voice makes my eyes open, even though I don't think my mind told them to. Well, I guess it had to because opening your eyes is a voluntary movement even though sometimes closing them isn't, like when someone shines a bright light directly at you and you have to protect yourself. The lady is looking at me. I have to answer. What was the question? Oh, right…. Is someone meeting me? Hardly.

"Um, no, I don't think so. I'll be fine though."

"Are you familiar with the city? If you need directions or even a ride, I can help out."

This lady is very nice. I do need directions and I do need a ride. I need a ride right back home where it's safe. I don't want to be here, in a strange place. I don't know where all of the streets are or what ones are direct. I like straight, direct streets. Sometimes they take a little longer to get me where I'm going, but I don't really like lots of curves and corners. I have a bad feeling that this city might be full of curves and corners, but maps aren't really very honest about that part of streets…they make everything look like a geometry assignment, all nice and clean when reality isn't like that at all.

"I'm fine." I already said that, but I can't think of anything else to say. I'm lying, but it's all right because "I'm fine" is one of those everyday lies that everyone tells. People are always saying "How are you?" and you are supposed to answer "Fine, thank you, and how are you?" even when you aren't fine at all. You're not supposed to say "I feel crappy today." Almost everyone says they're fine when you ask. They aren't all fine at all. It's just a good manners lie.

"All right then. It was nice meeting you."

"Yes, it was nice meeting you too." And there we go again. I don't think she really thinks that meeting me was nice. I didn't talk to her. All I did was breathe into her donut bag. And honestly, even though she was nice to me, it wasn't exactly nice meeting her. I would rather not have met her. Not meeting her at all would mean that I never got into the belly of a dragon.

Now that I've been spit out, I'm thinking maybe I'd be safer back inside. This bus station is nothing like the one back home. I knew it would be different because this is an actual bus station instead of just a store, but it's a lot more overwhelming than I expected it to be.

I didn't expect to see so many people walking around in

all directions, looking like they know where they're going. They all move pretty fast, and I press back against a wall so some man with a big suitcase on wheels doesn't mow me down like a bowling pin.

I like bowling. It's the only pseudo sport that I've ever had anything approaching fun playing. Five pin, not ten. I have small hands, especially for a boy. I didn't know there were gender specific rules about hand size, but adults in my life keep telling me that my hands are unusually small for a male. They seem to fit my arms and all ten digits work, so I don't think the size really matters much. Except when you talk about bowling. Ten-pin balls are large. I tried to pick one up once and it was painful, so I didn't try it again.

Five-pin balls fit very snugly into my hand. You only have to run a little before you can let go of the ball, and then you don't have to run again. No one is screaming at you to move because you stood there holding a bat, and the pitcher hit you in the leg with the ball, meaning you get to move to first base, but you don't understand why, and so you stand there while everyone yells. In bowling you're allowed to just stand there and watch as the ball hits the pins. If you line it up just right, you can hit an impressive array of pins.

The first time I bowled was pretty close to my last, though. People rent shoes to bowl. Seriously! Giving someone money to put germ-filled shoes on your feet. I mean, the balls are germy enough, but at least you can clean them off with your pocket-sized hand sanitizer. But shoes?

My mother was pretty sure that bowling was going to be

"my sport." This is because she already tried me in baseball, basketball, volleyball, swimming, and tennis. Baseball had too much running and yelling. Basketball had too much running and yelling. Volleyball had too much jumping and yelling. Swimming was too wet. Tennis had too much running and falling down.

Mom bought me my own shoes for bowling because there isn't much running, yelling, falling down, or getting wet in bowling. I liked bowling with my mother enough that she decided I should join a league with other kids.

I bowl in my living room on my Wii now. I'm really good at it, and no one groans when I miss a strike.

"Can I help you?"

I look up. I forgot for a moment that I'm still in a noisy, crowded bus station full of noisy crowds of people. Someone is standing in front of me. She has a blue blazer with a nametag on it which leads me to the brilliant deduction that she works here. *Miss Marple in the bus station with a nametag.*

"No, I'm fine."

I don't wait for her to find out that I manner-lied to her. I grab my bag against my stomach and try to move in one direction through the people moving in every direction. I need to find somewhere I can sit down and get my tablet out. There's a sign on the wall saying that there's free Wi-Fi in the bus station. I need to figure out where I am and how I'm going to start trying to find Angel.

I don't usually worry about things like how big I am or am not. Or what color my hair and eyes are or whether I'm fat or thin. I see my body as a container for my mind. So long as I feed it properly and keep it away from germs, I don't much care what it looks like. My mind is my most important part. It's my command center, keeping everything under control. My mind is usually a well-oiled machine, smoothly operating the rest of me.

But at this moment, I kind of wish I was taller so I could see where I'm going. This bus station seems to have been very specifically designed for tall people. All I can see is backs. I'm hoping one of them is heading for a quieter spot where I can sit down.

Finally I see a restaurant-type place on the right, with tables and chairs. I manage to push myself out of the flow of traffic and into the doorway. It's definitely quieter in here. There are only a few people sitting down. I move inside a bit so I'm not in the way and dig around in my bag. I need to buy something to eat or drink so that I can sit. I'm not really hungry because the diesel fumes on the dragon bus made me queasy, but a ginger ale would probably be a good thing. My mother always gives me ginger ale when my stomach is upset. She says it's a proven fact that the ginger in it has soothing properties. I suspect she didn't do thorough research on the topic, but I'll take her word for it this time.

I buy my ginger ale and move to a seat nearest the back wall. There are three extra chairs at my table, and I really hope that no one else decides to sit with me.

I pull out my tablet and turn it on. Angel told me the name of her friend and the name of her old school. That's all I have. It's probably not enough to go on, and I'm probably an idiot to be here trying to find her, instead of telling my mother and letting someone else do it.

My command center isn't doing such a good job. It must be getting rusty or something because my mind's gears are definitely not fully functioning right now.

What *am* I doing here? I don't know where I am or where I'm going or what I'm going to do next!

Calm down. Breathe in. Slowly, so you can control the germs. Hold it. Breathe out, making sure the bad stuff leaves and the good stuff stays. If there is any good stuff in this people-filled germ factory. No, don't think like that. Just breathe.

The screen glows at me. It's comforting and familiar. It looks the same no matter where I am. I open up Google Maps and type in the bus station. Martin Street. All right. So I'm on Martin Street. Now I know where I am. I just need to know where I'm going.

I have to figure out how to find Angel's friend. Angel said her name was Celina Abures. I wasn't particularly interested in her friend's name, but it stayed in my head anyway. Abures doesn't seem like that common a name, although I don't really know much about names or what ones are more common than others. I Googled my name once and got more than twenty million hits. I'm fairly certain that none of them were about me. Frederick Barry is not unique. Well, *I* am unique, but my name isn't.

Person Finder has three Abures families listed in this city. Figures.

I have to think. What else did Angel say about Celina that will help me? She talked so much to me that I'm sure I have about a million Angel words mushed up inside of my brain.

I think she told me once that she hates the bus to our school and that she used to be able to walk to school. Maybe she even said that she used to walk with Celina. I can't really remember, though. I might be just making it up because I don't know what else to do.

If she did walk to school with Celina, then logically the right Abures would be the one closest to the school.

The school's called Castleford Elementary School. Original. It's on Castleford Rd. Even more original. The city, the school, and the street all have the same name. Did someone run out of ideas?

I map the three addresses and find the closest one to the school. It is a bit closer to here than the other two addresses as well, which makes it the best choice on every level, but it still looks like a pretty far hike. I'm really not much into hiking.

I wish I had a car.

It wouldn't help me much because I don't know how to drive. Yet. I'm old enough to start lessons, but my mother isn't. I mean, she's old enough to drive but she isn't old enough for me to start lessons. She says she wants me to wait until I'm seventeen, even though she would really like me to wait until I'm twenty because the statistics on accidents and teenage boys are so terrifying that she'd like me to not be a teenage boy anymore when I start driving. Her logic is faulty in this, because I would imagine that I will be an equally bad driver at twenty as

I would be at seventeen, since my level of inexperience would be the same.

I drink the last of my ginger ale. My stomach is still sick. So much for the curative powers of over-processed ginger.

I'm not sure what I'm going to do when I get to Celina's house, anyway. Do I just go up and knock on the door and ask for Angel? Is that the polite thing to do in a situation like this? *Are* there situations like this, except for this one?

I stare at the map for another few minutes, memorizing the street names and directions I will have to turn in. I was right. I wish I had a data plan on my phone so that I could GPS it and have a nice voice talking me through the steps. My mother said it's too expensive and that Wi-Fi is good enough for a sixteen year old. I begged to differ, but she won, seeing as she pays for my phone plan.

The sidewalks are not as crowded as I was afraid they would be. There's more space out here than in the bus station, and the air feels a whole lot cleaner. I try to keep up a good, brisk walking pace but it's hard to do that when I'm scared of missing a turn. I have to keep my mind focused on the route so I don't forget where I'm supposed to go. I have to be careful not to let too many other thoughts in until I have the map permanently secured in my filing system.

I walk and walk. My feet are getting sore, but I keep going. If I stop I'll change my mind and head off in the other direction and beg a dragon to carry me home.

I'm focused on my feet and on the street signs, so I don't really see anything else. Because I'm so focused, Time is kind and passes quickly, leading the way to what I hope is Celina's house.

I'm here. Now what?

There's a bus shelter across the street with a bench in it. I can sit there and pretend I'm waiting for a bus. And while I sit, I'll try to figure out what to do next. And maybe, if I sit long enough, I'll figure out how I ended up in a bus shelter in a strange city, looking for an even stranger girl who somehow got me into this mess by telling me that friends don't tell.

I'm beginning to think that friends are highly overrated.

fourteen

Thirteen buses have passed by here. Seven buses have stopped and let people off or picked them up. Twenty buses altogether.

I don't think I've seen that many buses in one place in my whole life, except for this morning at the bus station. Big day.

I've been timing them, and they don't seem to have a very organized pattern. Sometimes there will be twenty minutes between buses and at other times thirty or thirty-six. They don't arrive at clean time intervals, like fives or tens. I like things to be in clean intervals. Multiples of five and ten are clean. Fours and sixes are not.

I haven't seen Angel or anyone who looks like she might be a Celina walk into the house across the street. I might have the wrong house.

If it is the wrong house, what am I going to do? I can't sit outside three houses at the same time. I can't sit here for three days looking for Angel. I was really hoping to make it home before school tomorrow morning, or my mother will get a phone call from the attendance robot and then there will be real trouble.

Somehow, I thought I'd be on my way home by now with Angel beside me, or at least some information about Angel *inside* me. That I'd sneak into my house and crawl into my own bed and everything would be normal again.

I thought this would all happen a whole lot faster than it seems to be happening. I don't know why I thought that. I'm pretty sure it isn't logical to think that. I have a very logical mind about most things. But I have no experience with this sort of thing. Is this a sort of thing? Is there a precedent for someone taking a bus to a strange city to find someone who seems to be missing even though she had a foolproof plan?

If I don't get back in time for school tomorrow, my mother will find out what I'm doing, and she will be angry with me.

I don't like anger. I try not to feel it because it's an uncomfortable and out of control feeling, as if my insides are turning red and molten with heat that burns my common sense until it melts and drips out of my mouth with words that I shouldn't say. When people are angry they say hurtful things. My mother's angry words always burn me, and it takes a long time for the scars to go away. I don't like to make her angry.

Finding out that I used money that she didn't know I have to take a bus to find Angel because I actually do have some idea of where she is even though I said I didn't, which is another big lie, will make her angry.

It's becoming increasingly obvious that I haven't really thought all of this through. I think my brain is melting. All of my life people have seemed so worried about me because I have never had many friends. *Any* friends except Robert, who is mostly an online friend, who doesn't expect much from me. I never worried about how many friends I did, or didn't, have. I never particularly wanted them. The whole friend thing seemed very complicated and tiring to me.

I was right. I am very tired. This *is* all very complicated. My head hurts from all of the uncontrolled thoughts swirling around. There aren't any colors in there at all right now. Only mud. Clear as mud, as my mother would say. Never understood that expression until right now.

It's getting late. No one has walked into that house yet.

I'm hungry. I haven't eaten anything all day. My stomach wasn't interested in food earlier when I was drinking my ginger ale. It's interested now.

I know I packed some granola bars in my bag so I start digging. I can't take my eyes off the house across the street, so I'm making a mess of my bag trying to feel around for them. I finally feel the crackly surface of the wrapper and pull my hand back out of the bag, trying not to spill everything else out on the bench.

The granola bar is crushed. All crumbs like a handful of oatmeal. I don't like eating crumbs. I know it's the same food as it was when it was all in one piece, but it won't feel the same in my mouth. I'm really hungry. But I don't like crumbs. I should have brought cereal. It's already in manageable pieces when you buy it.

Maybe I should just go home and confess to everything. I most likely can't make anything worse than it already is.

My phone is buzzing. I don't even look at it. That will be Mom calling me to see if I'm doing all right at Robert's house. I should answer her so she doesn't wonder, but if I answer, I'll have to lie. A big one. I don't want to lie again, and I'm not ready to tell her the truth. She'll be so angry. Either way.

I can't answer. I'll call her when I figure out what to say.

I'm hungry.

It's getting darker by the second. I don't want to sit here much longer. I'm not a big fan of the dark. It's unpredictable. It hides things from you. It keeps secrets.

"Hi."

The word startles me and I drop my bag on the ground. I didn't see anyone standing there because my eyes were focused on the house across the street. I take a quick look. I don't want to talk to a stranger in a bus shelter in a strange city.

It's a girl. A teen-aged girl who might be around Angel's age. It isn't Angel though. Of course not. That would be too easy.

"I've been watching you out my window. You've been here a really long time and any bus you might be waiting for has passed by here at least ten times. Are you lost or something?"

"Or something."

"Okay. Whatever. Do you need help? My parents aren't home yet, but they'll do something when they get here if you need them to." She points across the street at the house I've been staring at for hours. I never saw her go into the house or come out of it.

"Do you live there?" I point at the house also.

"Yes. Why?"

"Are you Celina?" She looks surprised that I know her name, which I guess makes sense. I suppose she wouldn't be expecting some random stranger who's hanging out in the local bus shelter to just happen to know who she is.

"Yeah. Why do you know my name? Why are you sitting in this bus shelter? Are you some kind of stalker or something?" She steps back so that the shelter glass is between us.

"I'm not a stalker. I'm looking for someone. I thought she would be here. She told me not to tell, but she told me you were in her plan, so telling you isn't really telling—is it?" She looks at me and shakes her head. People shake their heads at me a lot.

"I don't know what you're talking about. What friend?"

"Angel. She's missing because she was supposed to be coming here, and I'm trying to find her." Her eyes open wide and she puts her hand over her mouth. Her eyes fill up with tears and she shakes her head.

"I saw that on TV! She's missing, and it's probably all my fault." She starts crying and crying, tears pouring down her cheeks and snot pouring from her nose. I really want to be somewhere else, but I don't know where else to go at the moment.

"How could it be your fault?" I slide back a bit in case she sprays something on me.

"I told her not to come. At least I think I did. Maybe I didn't make it clear enough. I don't know. But she came, and I told her she couldn't stay, and she left. And I didn't do anything because I thought she'd just go home. I didn't tell anyone, and now the news says she's missing, and I still didn't tell anyone because I don't want to be in trouble, which makes me a bad person, but I don't really know where she is anyway, so what could I tell?"

She's sobbing and sniffing and talking at the same time and it's hard to understand her. Mostly it seems that she's as confused about the "don't tell" rules as I am.

"Well, she didn't go home or she wouldn't be missing." I speak calmly hoping it will calm her down.

"Obviously!" She shouts the word as me and I'm pretty sure some spit or snot landed on my arm.

"How am I supposed to find her now?" I'm not really asking her, but the words come out into the air anyway. She looks at me with her blurry red eyes. My arm is starting to itch.

"I have no idea. I have to go home now. I don't feel well." She starts crying again, hiccupping and sobbing all the way back to her house. I stand watching her for a couple of seconds.

That wasn't much help. Now what am I supposed to do? I'm in a strange city with nowhere to sleep and no one to talk to. I haven't got any idea where to look for Angel. If I even try, I'll probably get more lost than she is and end up missing too.

If I had a list of the world's stupidest ideas, me coming to Castleford to look for Angel would be at the very top. The Guinness World Record of stupid ideas.

I used to be so much smarter than this.

There's no choice. I have to go home. I have to walk back to the bus station in the dark and take another bus and then walk home in the dark and lie to my mother about where I've been and what I've been doing.

My mother calls it facing the music. I know what it means—owning up to something you did wrong and taking your consequences. But why is it called that? How do you *face* music? You can't see it, unless you have an oscilloscope and I don't think the expression is about sound waves. Maybe it's about being a conductor, who is someone who faces musicians who are *making* music…except you orchestrated a lie instead of a symphony.

Maybe I should be figuring out what I'm doing instead of wondering about strange expressions that my mother uses. I am beginning to wonder if I have a brain tumor or something that is stopping me from thinking clearly.

I retrace my steps, using the light from my tablet to help me navigate. The bus station is all lit up like a horizontal Christmas tree, and I'm so happy to be inside the light that I don't even mind all of the bodies. I check the schedule, and I haven't missed the second bus back home, which is leaving in about a half an hour. I think about buying myself a snack while I wait but looking at the food choices makes my stomach twist itself inside out, so I decide to just sit in the waiting area.

The dragon is less threatening on the way home. Or maybe I'm just too tired to notice him. I close my eyes for just a second, and when I open them again the bus is pulling into the parking lot. Ninety minutes just disappeared from my life without me even noticing.

It doesn't feel as dark here as in Castleford, even though

it's later. It's easy to find my way home, and I have my lie all ready by the time I reach the end of our street. It won't even feel like I'm lying because my mother won't have any trouble believing that I changed my mind about sleeping in a strange bed. That actually makes a lot more sense than the idea that I was prepared to spend the night at Robert's in the first place. I can put off having to face my mother's music for a little bit longer if she believes me.

I head around to the back of our house so I can come in the back door and through the kitchen. Just as I come around the corner into the yard, there's a flash of light over by Treehenge. It's too bright and too big to be a firefly, unless there's some kind of new giant bug out there flying around. I stand watching for a second. There it is again.

I walk toward the trees, but not too close. It's obvious to me now that someone is back there with a flashlight. Suddenly the light is shining in my face. I'm blinded for a second, so I can't see who's holding it.

"Kal? Is that you? It's about time you got here. I've been waiting for hours!"

FIFTEEN

Now I know what my dad means when he says someone looks like a deer caught in the headlights. Kal's eyes are so wide that his eyeballs look like they're going to fall right out and bounce across the ground. The thought makes me smile a little, even though life doesn't feel very funny right at the moment.

Life is mostly feeling stupid. Everything's all messed up.

I'm seriously hungry. I can smell the food coming from Kal's kitchen. *Kal's Kitchen*. Sounds like a reality show on the Food Channel.

Why am I thinking about food? The last thing I should be worrying about right now is filling my gut. I need to worry about the fact that I can't even go home.

Not yet, anyway. My parents called the cops about six seconds after I left, and now everything's turned into a big drama festival, and I'm going to be in major trouble, and I just can't face it right now.

I couldn't tell them the real reason I wanted to leave town. So I just made up a big excuse and hoped that someone would believe me. That someone would do something to help me get out of the mess I made of my life.

Except now I've made the pile of crap I'm living in even deeper by lying and running away, and I can't even start to dig my way out of it. There isn't even anyone around to give me a shovel.

Except Kal.

I don't have anywhere to go except here.

I thought I was going to be in Castleford by now, but it turns out that Castleford wouldn't be any better than here, anyway. Celina sure doesn't want me there. I spent about six minutes with her before I realized I had made a huge mistake.

"Angel, oh my God, what are you doing *here*?" Celina's voice squeaks on the last word. She looks completely shocked to see me, even though I told her I was coming.

"I told you. I'm going to stay with you for a while. You said it was cool."

She stares at me for so long that I start to wonder if there's something gross growing on my face that she's too polite to point out.

"I said it was a cool *idea*. I never said you should actually *do* it." She's shaking her head while she talks, just in case I don't understand the words.

"Actually, you did. You told me you missed me and thought it was cool that I was trying to move back here. You said I could stay here until my parents came and talked to me about it and understood how serious I was about moving." My stomach is starting to feel sick, and the headache that started on the bus just got ten times worse.

"No *way*. I never said that for real. I mean seriously, Angel, I could never ask my parents to have you come here if you're basically running away. They'd kill me if I got them involved with something like that. Besides, you know it would never work. You can't force parents to move. They're the ones in charge."

She's shaking her head again and just watching the movement is making me feel sicker. I have a sudden urge to punch her in the nose to make it stop.

She's lying. I know what she said to me. I still have the texts, which I could show her to prove it, but obviously it isn't worth the effort. There's nothing left to say. She's been lying to me the whole time. She never thought it was a good idea. She was never going to help me. She's just a chicken-shit imaginary friend who doesn't care about my problems.

Not that I actually told her my *real* problems. But that shouldn't matter. She should want to help me anyway. She is—*was* my friend.

I didn't bother saying anything else to her. My stomach was jumping around so much I figured I'd puke if I opened my mouth anyway. Then again, puking on her expensive new shoes might have been a good way to say good-bye.

Kal's the only one who has tried to help, and he's never even been sure he wanted me to be his friend. I've been working pretty hard to persuade him that I'm worth the effort, but I guess after this weekend, he's realizing that I'm not.

"Angel?" He's finally stopped his shocked staring routine and is whispering at me, which probably isn't necessary because we're pretty far from the house, and his mom's inside with the door shut.

"Hi." It feels like I should say more than that, but I don't know where to start.

"What are you doing here? Everyone is looking for you! You're missing!" He's still whispering but in the hissing, half-talking kind of way that makes him sound like a super villain or something. The thought of Kal as a super villain makes me laugh.

"Why are you laughing? This isn't funny. I had to go to the police station, and my mother is upset. Then I had to lie to her, which made me upset, and then I went to Castleford on a bus, which made me even more upset, and then you weren't there, and Celina cried, and I had to come home. And you're laughing."

I look at him. That's more than I think I've heard him say in the whole time I've known him. And it's not just the number of words. It's *what* he's saying. Kal can barely switch classes at school without having a panic attack. Why the hell would he go to Castleford on a bus?

"You went to Castleford? Why the *hell* would you do that?"

"I couldn't think of anything else to do. The police said you could be in trouble. The news said you could be in big trouble. You didn't call your parents like you said. You didn't answer your phone when I called you. You told me I couldn't tell. So I just went to find you. But you weren't there. You were here."

He shakes his head, looking confused. I can't believe he did that! It never occurred to me in a million years that Kal would get in any kind of trouble. I figured if things got too hot for him he'd just tell. That's what anyone else would do. Of course, Kal isn't like anyone else I know. But still, I would never *ever* have expected him to come looking for me.

"I'm so sorry. My phone died, and I didn't have anywhere to charge it once I got to Celina's."

"You didn't stay at Celina's. She said she sent you away. Then she cried. A lot." He screws up his face, making it obvious that crying is one of the things he finds disgusting. Kal finds a lot of things disgusting.

"Yeah, well, she *should* be crying. She seriously sucks at being a friend. She told me I could come and hang there, and then tried to tell me I didn't understand her or something stupid like that. I mean, I wasn't going to move in. I was just going to be there a couple of days or so. But she just boots me out. I still can't believe it. She was so supportive when we talked about it, all *we're BFF's, of course you can come.* The minute I show up, she pretends it never happened. And then she cries when you show up, pretending she's worried about me? She is so full of crap."

"Where did you go?" Kal asks.

"I didn't go anywhere at first. She has this weird little playhouse deal at the back of her garage that no one ever uses, so I slept there for the weekend. It was cold and smelled like feet. I threw up in the bushes behind it. I hope Celina stepped in it." Kal looks at me and shudders. I forgot that he doesn't like thinking about the grossness that comes out of our bodies.

"Do you want to borrow my phone so you can call your parents now?"

"I don't know what to say to them. I don't have a plan anymore." I can't believe that I thought this was going to work. That everything would just fall into place and my parents would come running to Castleford to rescue me and we'd live there happily ever after.

Kal looks at me like he wants to ask another question, but then he just nods. That's one of the things that I like about him. He usually doesn't ask me many questions unless he's practicing his conversation skills. He just kind of accepts the things I say. I'm usually not sure if that's because he thinks I know what I'm talking about or if he just isn't all that interested in what I'm saying most of the time.

"And so you came here."

"Yeah. I didn't know what else to do. I didn't want to be all alone, but I didn't want to go home. So here I am." I shrug my shoulders, trying to look like I'm cool about it all.

"You really can't live out here forever. It will get too cold in a couple of weeks."

"I won't still be here in a couple of weeks. I won't be here more than a couple of days." Hopefully.

"Your parents are worried. Your mother cried on TV."

"My mother cries a lot. She is not a happy person. I don't think my mother likes living here either. She misses her friends and her job back home. It's part of the reason

I thought I could persuade my parents to consider moving back. I thought Mom might possibly be on my side."

"Do you think my mother would cry if I was missing?" Kal asks this in a totally serious tone. Kal often wonders about things that the rest of us would think are obvious.

"Absolutely."

"Are you hungry?" Kal completely changes the subject a lot too. Sometimes it bugs me. Not this time.

"Very."

"I'll try to bring you some food later. First, I have to go in and lie to my mother."

"Okay. You do that, and I'll just wait out here." He nods and looks at me for a second.

"A blanket and a pillow too, I think. It's getting cold and your sweater doesn't look very warm."

"That would be good."

"Okay." He starts to walk toward the house but then stops and looks back at me.

"I didn't tell."

"I know. Thank you."

"You told me not to, so I didn't."

"I know. And I'm sorry it made trouble for you. Are the cops still bugging you?"

"I don't think so. I'm supposed to call them if I think of anything that would help find you."

"Can you hold off on calling them for me? Just give me a bit more time to figure out what to do?" He stares at me with those big serious eyes for a few seconds and then slowly nods his head.

"I won't tell unless you want me to." He looks at me for another second and then turns and walks away. I sit down to wait for him to come back, shaking my own head, which is starting to ache like crazy, which I totally deserve. This is all so messed up. I feel awful that I'm asking him to pretend he doesn't know where I am so that he's lying for me and talking to the cops for me. He's not that good with people most of the time, and this is probably incredibly hard for him to deal with.

I'm being a supremely shitty friend. I should just go home and let him off the hook. But if I go home, they'll want to know why I left. They'll want me to tell them the truth.

And I just can't.

SIXTEEN

"Angel?"

I'm relieved when I finally hear Kal whisper at me again. He's been gone a while and I was starting to worry that he wouldn't be able to figure out how to sneak back out of the house. I imagine he's not very good at that sort of thing.

"I brought you some stuff." He hands me a couple of granola bars, a banana, and a bottle of water. He sets a blanket and a pillow on the rock beside me and stands there looking at me. I can just barely see his face but I can tell he's feeling uncomfortable with everything.

"Thanks. Did everything go all right with your mom?"

"She believed me. I'm not sure if that's all right or not. She's gone to sleep now so she doesn't know I left."

"Sorry you have to keep lying for me. I'll get out of your way as soon as I can."

"That would be a good idea." He turns to head back to the house. That's it? He's not even going to say good night? I haven't talked to anyone for almost two days.

"Kal? Could you stick around for a bit and talk to me? It's kind of dark and lonely out here. I know it's a lot to ask." Everything I've asked him to do is a lot. Too much.

"It is a lot to ask. It's late and I'm tired. I have school in the morning and I like to have at least seven hours of sleep. I won't get that if I stay here." I shine my light toward his back. He doesn't even turn around.

He's right. I should just suck it up and leave him alone.

"*Please*? Just for a few minutes?"

He stands there silently for a few seconds, probably trying to figure out if I'm worth the effort or not. Finally he shrugs and turns to face me.

"Just for a few minutes. And don't shine your flashlight in my face."

"Okay. Great. Thanks. Um, so what do you want to talk about?"

"Me? I don't know. This is your idea. You decide."

"Okay. Well, I don't want to think about the mess my stupid life is in right now, so maybe we could talk about the past. You know, get to know each other better. Share life stories."

"If you want to." He sounds tired. I should just shut up and let him go to bed.

But I don't.

"Great. Let me think. Oh, I know. Did you know I used to have a pet unicorn?"

"A *what*?" That woke him up a little.

"When I was a kid I thought I had a pet unicorn. Seriously. It was in my bedroom in the house we lived in about six or seven houses ago. I totally loved that bedroom. My mother made it for me. It had this fantasy wallpaper on the bottom half, all covered with scenes of princesses and castles and knights and dragons. Every night I would stare at them and imagine I could actually fly off the bed and into the wallpaper and when I fell asleep I would dream about them all night long. I was always the princess, of course, a beautiful princess with long, silky blonde hair and perfectly straight teeth. As I'm sure you know, all true princesses have straight teeth so that they have perfect smiles to win the hearts of the brave princes who come to slay the dragons. Except in my dreams there wasn't any dragon slaying because I've always liked dragons."

"I don't really like dragons. They're too full of fire."

"That's one of the things I like about them. Anyway, the top half of the walls was painted a crazy bright purple and had pictures of unicorns all over it that my mother had cut out of a calendar someone gave me for Christmas. Sometimes, when no one else was looking, the unicorns would fly down to the bottom half of the wall and hang out with the dragons and princesses. It was better than TV."

"Paper unicorns would fly?" I look over at him and smile a little. At least he's listening.

"Well, I helped them a little. But then, one day I came into my room and discovered that one of the unicorns had decided to jump down off of the wall and become completely real. I wasn't even scared. That was partly because I was four and didn't think there was anything strange about a unicorn standing in my room, and partly because I knew that unicorns wouldn't hurt me."

"You do know that unicorns aren't real, right?" Kal's voice sounds a bit worried and I when I shine my light toward his feet, I notice that he's taken a couple of steps backwards. Probably afraid my insanity might be contagious.

"He sure seemed real to me that day. He was awesome. His horn was silver and sparkly, like tinsel on a Christmas tree when the lights are on. He looked at me, and I think he was smiling, although it's hard to tell with unicorns. I walked up to him and petted him very gently the way my mother had taught me to pet animals. He rubbed his nose against me and I reached out and touched his horn. The second my finger made contact, he just disappeared."

"That's probably a good thing."

"I didn't think so. I wanted him to come back. I told my mother all about it and she told me it sounded very wonderful but that most people didn't believe that unicorns are real, so it should be our little secret. I didn't believe her. How could people think that unicorns aren't real when there was one standing on my floor? But I usually listened to my mother, at least back then, so I shut up about him."

"Mothers are right sometimes."

"Yeah, I found that out in grade two when my teacher, Mrs. Laraby, did something I thought was totally amazing. She showed us this big book filled with photographs of unicorns. I couldn't believe my eyes! My mother told me to stop believing in them and here was a teacher showing us pictures of them. Photographs—real live photographs of real live unicorns, not some pretend drawings. Big, beautiful, white unicorns just like the one that visited me. I was so excited to think that maybe Mrs. Laraby believed in unicorns too. Even though she never actually said that unicorns were real. She said that she just wanted us to think about it. She asked us to think about what made things real. She asked us if we believed there was such thing as a million dollars, which of course we all did, but then she asked us if anyone had ever actually seen a million dollars, which, of course, none of us had. I didn't know what a million dollars had to do with unicorns, but I didn't care. I was just so excited that someone had made a book that proved unicorns were real and that my mother was wrong to tell me to shut up about them.

I remember putting my hand up and opening my mouth and telling everyone about the unicorn that came into my room when I was little. And I remember some of the boys starting to laugh like crazy. I could feel my face getting red, and my eyes started stinging like they wanted to cry. But I laughed instead, pretending that I was just kidding and told the boys they were pretty stupid to have believed me. Then everyone started laughing at them, instead. Mrs. Laraby ended up yelling at everyone and putting the book away. That was the day I realized my mother was right, after all. No one thought that unicorns were real, even though the teacher showed them to us in a book."

"I don't think that unicorns are real." Kal's voice comes at me out of the dark. I almost forgot he was here for a second.

"You already said that. I guess most people don't. Not even me anymore. It's kind of weird when you think about it. When you're small, everyone else tells you to believe in random things that you can't see, like tooth fairies and Easter bunnies. I thought that rabbits laid eggs for years until someone explained it all to me. But try to find your own unicorn, and suddenly you have to shut your mouth and grow up. So I stopped thinking about unicorns and just kept on pretending that some fat guy squeezed down our chimney every December for the next few years, until I was told I wasn't supposed to believe in him, either."

"It has been my experience that adults think they're boss of everything, including your imagination. You don't get to pick what you believe in."

"Exactly. It sucks, right? I mean, who are they to tell us what to think just because they're old? I've never told that story to anyone before because I figured no one would understand. But you do...sort of anyway. Okay, now it's your turn."

"My turn for what?"

"Tell me a life story."

"I don't think I have any. I've never had a unicorn, or any other mythical creature, living in my bedroom. I never believed in Santa Claus or the tooth fairy because the idea of someone handing presents to every child in the world one night a year is completely illogical, not to mention the idea that there's a fairy flying around taking children's teeth."

"You thought it was illogical when you were four? You *knew* the word *illogical* when you were four?"

"As far as I can remember."

"Maybe that *is* your life story."

"Does that mean I can leave and go to bed now?" He sounds so happy at the thought of getting away from me that I have to take pity on him.

"I guess so. I know you need your beauty sleep."

"I don't see what sleep has to do with beauty, but I do need to get at least seven hours."

"You'd better hurry then. Sorry I kept you out here. I'm cool now. Thanks for listening."

"You're welcome. My mom leaves early for work, so I can come and get the blankets and things and bring you breakfast before I leave for school."

"That would be great. Have a good sleep."

"Good night."

He walks away and I'm left alone, sitting on a rock with nothing but my key chain flashlight to keep me company. I'm sure Kal is glad to be back inside his warm and clean house. I don't imagine I look very sanitary to him at the moment. I think I can actually smell myself and it isn't very pretty.

I imagine I both look and smell like shit at the moment.

Not that I'm exactly gorgeous the rest of the time. Not like the girls at school that all the guys think are so hot with their straight hair and straight teeth and straight bodies that don't have any lumps or bumps in the wrong places.

I'm not very straight. Most things about me are crooked. Personally, I've always tried to think that it makes me more interesting.

My hair is a crooked mess because it's super curly. Not

the beautiful kind of curly that most actresses and models have, which is a bit of a problem, seeing as I want to be an actress someday. My hair is fuzzy, frizzy, steel-wool curly. My mother used to work really hard to keep it under control when I was little. Tight braids that hurt like crazy. She gave up on it a few years ago though. Now my hair is in control and it likes to go all over the place.

My teeth are also crooked. My top ones stick out over my bottom ones. Like a beaver. Which is one of the things I get called a lot. Now that I'm fifteen and definitely fully grown, it's time to get braces. I don't want them because it looks like they hurt, but my mother says that straight teeth will be good for me. It will help my self-esteem.

Self-esteem is basically the way you measure how good you feel about yourself. Apparently the higher it is, the better you feel about who you are and what you look like. I know some girls at school whose self-esteem levels are off the charts. They love themselves totally and treat everyone else like shit.

Maybe it's better to have lower self-esteem and a nicer personality.

I actually have never really had a problem with my self-esteem, at least not until recently. I've never measured it, but I would guess it's usually somewhere in the middle of whatever weird scale is used to figure it out. My mother has always been a lot more worried about my looks than I am. Maybe my problem is low *mom*-esteem. She wants me to be someone different and will only feel better about me if I straighten myself out.

She doesn't just want me straighter. She'd like me to be smaller too. As in "Don't you think you should try to lose a few pounds? It will make you feel better about yourself." My body isn't crooked so much as lumpy, with some of the lumps in the wrong place like my belly instead of my boobs. In other words, I'm fat. Not like super huge, can't-walk-down-the-hall fat. Just more flesh than is socially acceptable: don't-look-good-in-boot-cut-jeans fat. My mother is very skinny. She watches everything she eats and exercises like crazy. She thinks I should do that too. I guess she's not totally wrong. I mean, it would be easier to look more like her. Probably be fewer girls pissing on me and more guys interested in me. I think about it sometimes. Imagine what it would be like to fit into smaller clothes, which might make me fit in better at school. I wonder if that's where they get that expression? But it just seems like so much work. All that dieting and running around going nowhere. And then what if I lose the weight and nothing changes anyway?

Not that any of that matters anymore. No one is thinking about my weight at the moment. They're just wondering where the hell I am.

Everyone but Kal, who keeps getting deeper and deeper into my pile of shit with me just because he didn't run fast enough when I came after him trying to be his friend.

I know it's a mistake to be sitting here behind Kal's house, instead of going home. I know I have to leave him alone and just make myself go home and try to clean up my mess.

But I just can't do it right now.

I know I'm being a total selfish bitch and a crappy friend…but I just need a little more time.

I'll be safe here until tomorrow.

I know Kal won't tell anyone.

SEVENTEEN

It's so dark out. How did it get so dark? What time is it?

Better question: Where am I?

I can feel a hand under my shirt. It's not mine. Why is there a hand under my shirt?

I can feel fingers fighting with the waistband of my jeans, twisting and turning the fabric until the metal fastener digs into my skin. I know I should be reacting to what's happening here, but I can't seem to get my mind moving fast enough to do anything. I still can't really figure out what's going on.

I feel like I'm going to puke. My stomach starts to heave and I can taste sour beer in the back of my throat. The panicky feeling of being afraid that I'm going to vomit somewhere embarrassing takes over, and for a second I'm six years old and throwing up on all of the nice people waiting in line at some amusement park my father took us to.

"Can't you at least give me some warning first?" he asked reasonably, as he hustled me out of line while trying to apologize to all the disgustingly smelly people. He didn't yell, but I started to cry anyway. Maybe because I was going to miss out on the ride.

Why am I thinking about that when the hand is still moving up my body and reaching under my bra? I don't even know whose hand it is. My mind isn't working. I try to focus on the face attached to the body that owns the hand.

"Eric?" I breathe the name out, trying not to spew out beer and peanuts along with the syllables.

"What are you doing?" I try to sit up, struggling out from under his weight, as I realize that he is lying on top of me, both hands busy as he laughs. I manage to focus on his face and see that he isn't even smiling. The laugh is coming from somewhere else.

"You know what I—we're—doing. Don't play dumb." His voice is soft, gentle even, as if we're having a romantic moment that we both want.

"Get off me! I don't know what you're talking about! Leave me alone!" My voice rises until I'm screeching. He looks startled and then disgusted. His face looks exactly like the people I puked on at the amusement park.

"Don't scream. What the hell is your problem?" His voice punches into my head. I can feel the tears starting down my face, which makes him even angrier.

"What are you crying about? We were just having a good time. You wanted to come here." He shakes his head and stands up. I'm still down on the ground, stomach heaving as tears and snot fight for domination over my face.

"This is bullshit. She's not worth anything, man. Let's just get out of here. You didn't do anything wrong. Let's just go." Another guy walks over, and looks down at me like I'm a piece of dog crap that he just scraped off his shoe. I recognize him. He's Peter Murphy, the guy Kal calls a Despiser. It was his laughter I heard. He must have been watching. Maybe waiting his turn. He's got his phone in his hand. Was he recording?

"It's pretty late and she's obviously still drunk."

"So?"

"I don't know. If she gets hurt or lost or attacked or something, it'll be on us." Eric shrugs and looks at me, shaking his head.

"It's not our fault she freaked out. She can take care of herself. Let's just get out of here. Come on."

Eric looks at me again. He hesitates for just a second and I think maybe he's going to help me up and clean me off and tell me it was all a mistake. That he thinks I'm cute and that he'll walk me home and see me tomorrow.

By the time I finish the thought, he turns around and runs off into the night.

I sit up, wiping my nose on my sleeve. I look around. I'm in some kind of field. I don't know where. I don't know how far I am from the party we were at. I've only lived here a couple of months, and I don't really know my way around. I have no idea where my house is from here.

We were at a party. I can't even remember whose party. I was just so happy to be invited. The last thing I remember *doing was laughing at Eric as I showed him how well I could chug a beer without taking a single break to breathe. Everyone seemed pretty impressed. I didn't tell anyone that I had never chugged anything but milk before.*

No one from the party knows I'm here. No one would even care. My parents think I'm at a sleepover party with some girls from school. As if.

I push myself to my feet and sway a little. He said I'm drunk. Am I? I've never actually been drunk. I had a couple of drinks with Celina last year, but I was always afraid to go any further than that. Celina told me I'm a control freak about booze and that I'm afraid I'll say or do something stupid if I have more than two drinks. That I'm missing out on a lot of fun because I'm so uptight.

I wonder what she'd think of me now.

My head is alternating between spinning and pounding. I feel like Eric punched me in the head with his fists, instead of just words. My stomach starts to heave and I lose control of it along with the rest of me.

Now I know what it means when someone says "I puked my guts out". There can't be any more food or booze down there, so I must be losing body parts by now. Maybe I'll lose some weight.

Emptying out the a week's worth of stomach contents seems to be helping a little, so I risk standing up and trying to figure out where I am. I quickly close my eyes for a second as I try to stop what little I can see of the world from dancing around me. It's hard enough to figure out where I am without everything constantly moving.

It's so dark. So much can be hiding in the blackness. I have to move or something could happen to me.

Something else could happen to me.

My hand strays up under my own shirt, feeling my stomach and wondering how much happened before I woke up enough to know where I was. I don't know what I said or did. I obviously did something to make him think I wanted to make out with him. I must have been so drunk that I completely lost control over my brain.

I feel sick. I think I'm going to throw up again.

I feel stupid. So stupid.

I actually thought he liked me. That things were starting to turn around. That my luck was finally changing, and I had stopped spraying myself with guy repellent. That life here really was going to be different. That my parents were right when they told me I would get used to it and make some friends.

I just made a total fool of myself with a guy I go to school with while another guy I go to school with probably caught it on his phone. He's probably posting it right now.

I'm standing in a field with puke on my shoes and snot in my hair. My life is completely over.

I can't tell anyone about this. Ever.

I hate this place.

I just want to go home.

"Angel?" Kal's voice interrupts my nightmare.

"Over here!" I shake off the memory as much as I can before facing him. I don't want him to read anything in my face.

I'm not ready to tell him about it. I might never be. I don't even like telling myself about it, but I can't seem to stop it replaying in my mind, over and over like some kind of bad commercial that keeps interrupting the hockey game.

What am I worrying about? This is Kal. He wouldn't notice if I shaved my head and grew a beard.

"Did you sleep?" He looks worried, like he's afraid he's been a bad host or something.

"Not really. The pillow and blanket were nice and all, but it was just so dark and noisy out here. Animals make a lot of noise at night. Don't they know it's sleep time?" I try a smile. He looks back at me seriously.

"Lots of animals are nocturnal. That means they sleep during the day."

"Yeah, I know what it means. Thanks though." I'm pretty sure he thinks I have the brain of a six year old. I guess most people do, compared to him.

"You're welcome. I brought you some breakfast. My mom will be leaving for work soon, so you can sneak in and wash up and things." He hands me a peanut butter sandwich and a glass of juice. He's standing so far back that he has to stretch his arms out to reach me, probably because he thinks I'm unsanitary at the moment. I resist the sudden urge to grab him in a bear hug. I can't afford to scare him away right now.

"Thanks. I'm actually hungry, which is too bad because I haven't had much appetite recently, and I think I've been losing weight. Not that it matters anymore because I can't ever go out in public again." He looks confused, like he always does when I talk about weight. Actually, Kal looks confused when I talk about most things. He's the smartest person I know, but I still think I'm a mystery to him most of the time. What can I say? I'm complicated.

"Why not?"

"Oh, no reason. I'm just being stupid." I can't explain it to him. Can't tell him that I think some guy has a video of me drunk and making out with some other guy in the woods that he's probably already shared with half the kids at school. I can't show my face in this town again. It was hard enough to get through those four and a half days, just waiting for the bomb to explode in my face. Nothing happened, which in a weird way made it all much worse because it just felt like they were torturing me, making me wait for the ultimate humiliation.

"I don't think you're actually stupid."

"You don't?"

"No. I don't think you're as smart as me, but you have your own kind of intelligence. You know about friends and things."

"I don't actually know much about friends. I don't seem to have one anymore, except you. And I managed to get you in all kinds of trouble and made you go all the way to Castleford for nothing."

"That's true."

"Great. I'm glad you agree that I'm a lousy friend."

"I didn't agree to that. I don't think you're a lousy friend. I don't know enough about friends to give you any kind of adjective. Are you going home soon?" He does his instant subject-change routine, which is probably a good thing right now.

"I don't know what to do. I guess I have to go sometime."

"Do you want to do it now?" Guess he wants to get rid of me before his mom finds me back here.

"Maybe later today. I'd like to grab a shower and get cleaned up a bit before I go, if that's still okay."

"Sure. I'll come back out and tell you when my mom's gone. It should be any minute now." He looks at his fancy diver's watch that he bought, even though he doesn't know how to swim. Kal is pretty complicated too.

He walks back to his house without saying anything else. I've never met anyone like him before. He seems to forget to end conversations, just wandering off in the middle of them when he thinks of something more important that he should be doing. My mom would call it rude, but it doesn't really feel rude when Kal does it. It just feels…like Kal.

I feel like a total jerk for what I've done to him. Kal is kind of—I don't know the right word—*innocent*? Close enough. He lives in some type of bubble where he's just floating around watching the rest of us as if we're interesting zoo animals or something. You can tell him pretty much anything when it comes to feelings and things like that, and he'll believe you. He doesn't really seem to understand emotions very well. I think he has some but they're hiding inside the bubble where the rest of us can't see them.

He has enough problems at school without me adding to them with all of my drama. I should have just kept him out of it. Now I have him lying and talking to the cops and sneaking around his own house. I should just give him a break and get out of his face.

I have to make myself go home and face whatever crap they're going to shove at me. And I have to do it now, before he comes back and I change my mind.

I'll just stick to the trees so no one sees me. Eventually I have to come out on some kind of a road—I hope.

I seriously doubt he's going to be too upset if I'm not here when he comes back.

EIGHTEEN

I move into the woods fast so I'm far enough away that when Kal comes out he won't spend time looking for me. Kal is like the attendance champion of our school, always there and always on time. There's no way he's going to risk losing that for me.

I'm not sure what direction I'm taking. The whole north-south-east-west thing doesn't really mean much to me. My father always tells me to look at the sun, so I can figure out what way is west. I'm not sure why it's useful to try to head west, but at the moment I don't know what else to do, so I try to move toward the sun, which is shining in my eyes and giving me a giant headache.

Not as bad as after the party though. That was the worst headache of my entire life, just pounding and pounding like some kind of psycho drummer got loose inside my brain.

Every time my head pounded, my stomach heaved, and I felt like I was going to puke. I kept kneeling down and praying to the toilet bowl, but nothing wanted to come up, so I just lay on the bathroom floor, crying for most of the morning.

The only good part about feeling so sick was that it blurred my memory of the night before for a while. All I could think about was not dying from the pain and nausea.

After a few hours I managed to drink some water and take some pain pills without feeling like I was going to spew them across the room. My head started to clear, and that's when the memories started.

"Hey, I know you. You're Angie or something like that, right?"

I'm standing at a table covered in open beer bottles in a room in a house that belongs to someone I don't even know. One of the girls in my gym class told me there was an open party Friday night, and that I should come. She gave me the address and everything, so I thought she really wanted me there. I was sick of sitting at home watching sports on TV with my dad every Friday night, so I told my parents I was going to a girl's sleepover party. I figured that way I wouldn't have a curfew and they wouldn't be watching for me to come home. Seemed really smart at the time. My mother was so pathetically happy that someone actually invited me to her house that she just let me go, no questions asked.

Very irresponsible of her.

"Angel."

"Seriously? Like with wings and all that? That's cute."
He smiles at me and suddenly my name seems like the best

one in the world as my stomach fills up with a zillion but-terflies crashing into each other. I know him. Eric Laplante. Grade eleven and the cutest guy in the school. I watch him sometimes when we're in the library at the same time, and I'm sure he can't see me looking. Stalker crush.

"I guess. Kinda lame." I try a smile, hoping I don't have popcorn stuck in my teeth. I grab a beer and take a big gulp to try to rinse out my mouth just in case. It tastes gross, and I have to force myself not to spit it out on Eric's shoes. How does my father drink this stuff?

"Hey, a beer drinker. Girl after my own heart!" Eric grabs a beer and starts drinking it. I know I'm staring, but I can't help it. He's just pouring it down his throat like he's the kitchen sink.

"Come on, finish it up," he says, putting his hand over mine and guiding my bottle back to my mouth. The but-terflies start swarming, turning into something much louder, like bees, and I feel like everyone can hear my stomach panic along with the rest of me. I put the beer to my mouth and just force it down, keeping my mouth open and pouring it straight down my throat, like I used to with milk when I was a kid. You get rid of it faster and don't have to taste it as much that way.

"Awesome! And kinda cute too. Try it again!" He looks impressed and I silently thank my mother for forcing so much milk on me. I try it again, just to keep him talking to me. The next hour is a blur of butterflies, bees, and beer.

And the next thing I remember after that is the field and Peter Murphy's ugly laugh.

Remembering the feeling of Eric's hands under my shirt makes my skin crawl, and I have trouble sleeping at night, wondering what really happened and what could have happened, if I hadn't stopped him when I did. The idea that Peter Murphy was watching, and probably recording everything, eats away at my brain. My head hurts at the thought of how much everyone will enjoy watching "The Whore Show," starring Angel Martinez.

No boy has ever wanted to kiss me before. I've never been on a real date. I thought the first time someone put his hand under my shirt it would be my boyfriend, and it would be beautiful and romantic. I used to stare at Eric and wonder what it would be like to have someone like him want to be with someone like me. Now I know.

It's awful.

He didn't really want to be with *me*. He just wanted to be with someone who had boobs and too much booze. He didn't care about *me* at all. Not for one tiny second.

I felt—feel—dirty and stupid and embarrassed and scared. I had to get away from everyone and everything that reminds me of what a mess I've made.

A branch smacks me in the face, reminding me that I haven't exactly stopped making messes. Now I'm wandering around in a forest that is way bigger than it looked from the outside and doesn't seem to have any friendly fairies or unicorns around waiting to show me the way. I forgot my knapsack back at Kal's place, with my keys and, therefore, my flashlight in it. So I have to find my way out of here some time in the next ten hours or so, before it gets dark, and I'm even more seriously screwed than I already am.

All trees look the same to me, and they're all too tall. I keep losing sight of the sun and I have no idea if I'm heading west. I don't even know if the stupid sun is even in the west this time of day. I also have no idea what direction my house is in from here so it probably doesn't make much difference. All I need to do is get out of all this nature and find a nice paved road that actually leads somewhere useful.

I'm getting hungry again. I would be a much thinner person if I didn't get hungry so often. I don't have any food, so maybe I'll be a much thinner person anyway, if I can't find my way out of these trees. My mother would be so pleased.

"Angel!"

I think I hear someone calling my name but it's faint and I'm probably imagining it. No one knows I'm out here but Kal, and he's at school by now, probably telling his math teacher how to do last week's homework.

"Angel!"

There it is again. I'd better stop moving until I'm sure I'm not just hearing things. I hope it's Kal and really hope it isn't at the same time.

"Angel!" Louder now and obviously Kal's voice. The attendance champion is skipping school to find the loser of the week.

Shit.

I just made everything worse.

NINETEEN

"Kal!" I yell as loudly as I can and wave my arms. I'm not sure what good that's doing, though. He won't be able to see me buried in this mess of branches that are doing their best to keep me hidden. If I try to move and find some sort of clearing, I'll probably end up going in the wrong direction, and he'll never find me. I don't want him wandering around looking for me forever.

"Hi." His voice comes at me from behind. Obviously the branches are no match for Kal's super brain.

"Hi. Fancy meeting you here." Lighten the mood a bit.

"I was looking for you," he says in a confused voice that makes it obvious he doesn't find me very funny.

"I figured. You shouldn't have been. Now you're missing school."

He looks at his watch, panic jumping into his eyes.

"I didn't think you'd be this far away. You move faster than I thought you would."

"You mean for a fat girl?"

"I didn't say that. I'm having trouble also, and I'm thin."

He does look winded. His cheeks are all red, and I think I actually see moisture on his forehead. This is the first time I've ever seen him sweat. I guess thin people aren't always in good shape, after all.

I know he meant "for a fat girl" but he's probably afraid to say it because I keep giving him shit when he does, which probably isn't totally fair to him. When I first met Kal, I was pissed off with him every time he called me fat or chubby. It took me a while to realize that he isn't actually trying to be mean when he says those things. He's really just analyzing the situation. It's still hard not to feel offended when the words pop out of his mouth, but I have to make myself shake it off.

"How did you find me?"

"I could see some broken branches and I figured that's where you started off, and then I just went in a straight line and listened. You aren't a very quiet walker."

"Oh. Well, now you found me, you can go home and get to school and live your life."

"Why did you leave without telling me?"

"I decided I was becoming a supremely shitty friend. I feel like a total jerk for what I've done to you."

"But you need to come with me. We need to go back to my place so you can figure everything out."

"I need to go home and figure out my own life." I'm still not sure if I'm going home yet, but there's no point in telling him that.

"I don't think your house is in this direction. It's safer for you to come back to my house and then go home from there."

He's probably right. Plan A was to stick to the forest so I could sneak my way home, but the trees aren't very helpful. Everyone is at work or school by now anyway, so the roads are probably the best way to go. Street signs are a lot more useful than the sun for finding my way home.

"Okay. You can show me which way to go." He looks surprised that I agreed so fast.

"All right. Well, the most logical thing would be to go back the way we came. I am reasonably certain that we walked in a straight line." He turns and starts walking so I follow. He's not going very fast, and he keeps stopping every few seconds to stare at the trees and bushes.

"It would be so much more efficient if eyes didn't have to work together as a team," he says, stopping so suddenly that I bump into him. He jumps away from me as if I burned him with a hot poker.

"What are you talking about?"

"Eyes. They move together. It would so much more effective if we could move each one on its own. I could look down at my feet with one and up at the trees with the other and we could move much more quickly." He starts rolling his eyes around. He's right. They do move together. He looks a little demented, and I wonder if he's starting to lose it.

"I had a friend once with what she called a lazy eye. It used to move off to the side when the other eye was standing still. That was creepy." I start rolling my eyes around, too, until it starts to make me dizzy.

"I don't think that's what I'm talking about. If I could control my eyes individually at school, I could read something interesting and watch for the teacher at the same time." Now he's going cross-eyed, looking down at his own nose.

"Yeah, and you could work on the computer and watch for Despisers at the same time—eliminate the element of surprise. Then we could eliminate them!" I laugh at my own funniness. He doesn't. He's still making weird faces, trying to control his eyes.

"I can't do it. Physically impossible." He gives up and looks disappointed. He turns and starts walking again without saying anything else. Guess the break is over.

We keep on starting and stopping our way through the woods for a really long time. My legs are beginning to ache and my feet are complaining. It's taking a lot longer to get back than it did to get this far, and for the first time I'm starting to wonder if Kal the Super Brain actually knows what he's doing.

"I guess we're walking a lot slower now."

He stops at the sound of my voice, looking surprised that I'm still back here. "What?" He seems distracted.

"I said, I guess we're walking slower. That must be why it's taking so long." I take advantage of him stopping to flop down on the ground and catch my breath for a few seconds.

"That's one possibility but not the most likely one." He looks up at the treetops. I look up, too. I wonder what we're looking for.

"Okay. That doesn't sound great."

"No. It isn't very great at all. I think that we are lost." His head moves from side to side, as if he's waiting for an idea to jump out at him.

"Lost? In the woods? How could we be lost? You *found* me. You can just retrace your steps and get us back. You're smart. Smart people can do stuff like that." My voice is getting louder and higher, which gets all of the birds excited, so that they join in.

Kal makes a pissed-off face at me and closes his eyes. "I *am* smart. I just don't know much about orienteering, and I don't have the sound of your walking to help guide me now."

"Orienteering?"

"It means navigating the woods. More or less. I've read about it in books but never researched it because it never really interested me. I don't usually go any farther than Treehenge."

"Treehenge?" I sound like a parrot. No wonder the birds are excited.

"It's what I call the spot behind my house. It's like Stonehenge only with trees. Stonehenge is a place…"

"I know what Stonehenge is!" My mother makes me watch a lot of BBC shows with her.

"Anyway, calling it Treehenge was my special joke, and now I accidentally told you." He shakes his head, opening his eyes and looking at me sadly.

"Well, don't look so bummed about it. It kind of takes the funny out of the joke. I wish we were there right now."

"I wish that, too. I'm not sure how to find it, though. I thought we were just going back the way we came, but if that was true, we would be there by now even allowing for our much slower pace." He looks at his diver's watch. Too bad he doesn't have a lost-in-the-woods watch that could tell us where to go.

"So, what do we do?"

Kal looks confused for a second. It's not a good look on him.

"I have to sit and think for a bit. Maybe I can find some information."

"Find some information? Where? We don't have Wi-Fi out here."

"I meant in my mind. I have a lot of information stored up there and sometimes I have to search for it for a while before I can access it."

"So, you're saying your brain is a computer and now you just need to literally google yourself?" I laugh at my own extreme funniness, but he just looks at me completely seriously.

"Of course. Everyone's brain is a computer. An actual computer is just an artificial attempt to replicate a human brain. Our brains can do everything a computer can and so much more. People made computers not the other way around."

"Well, compared to yours, my brain is more like one of those old-fashioned typewriters than a computer. Type stuff in, but nothing much comes out." That sounds pathetic, even to me.

"That's not true. Your brain is every bit as much a computer as mine. You just use it differently, so people call me smarter than you. It's just another label. It doesn't mean anything, really."

"I don't know about that. Most people think that smarter is better."

"Lots of people think I'm smart, but I don't think too many people think I'm better than they are. At least not at school."

That's a really good point. Which proves how much smarter he is because I never would have thought of that.

"So what makes one person better than another? Why do the kids at school bug you because you're smart and other people because they're not?"

"My mother says that kids who bug are the ones with the problem."

"When they're bugging me it sure feels like *I* have the problem. I've had all of the lectures from my mother about it. *Bullies are cowards. Bullies can't hurt you if you don't let them. Always tell on bullies so that you can make them stop. Stand up to bullies.*" I do a really bad impression of my mother, which would royally piss her off if she could hear me.

"My mother basically told me the same things."

"Yeah, well, bullies *are* cowards, but sometimes they're really big, strong, and mouthy cowards who can still make life hell. Bullies always find ways to hurt you. Telling on a bully just makes things worse. Standing up to bullies only works if you're bigger, smarter, or have a whole lot of people standing behind you when you do it."

"The only thing you can do with bullies is to try not to let them get inside your head."

"If you can do that, you're lucky. It isn't so easy. Bullies are just so stupid. The *word* is stupid. It doesn't describe the kind of person that does the shit they do. It's just too silly."

"I think that lots of words are silly. And right now, I think we need fewer words so that I can have some quiet and try to figure out what to do."

Which is a very polite way of telling me to shut up. So I do.

I really don't get how it all works. Some kids are just the ones who do the tormenting and others are just the ones who get tormented. There are smart kids who get picked on and other smart kids who do the picking. There are not so smart kids who get picked on and not so smart kids who do the picking. The same with attractive versus not so attractive kids.

Mostly though, smart, slim, and good-looking with enough money for cool clothes seems to be a good combination to have at school. Teachers and other kids like you better.

Kal is smart. He's not bad looking, just a little weird. He's really skinny, and his hair looks like he cut it himself. His pants are too short, and he always wears shirts that have weird pictures on them like X-Men and things that usually stay back in grade school. He has really nice eyes when he lets you see them, and he looks almost cute when he smiles every once in a while.

Kal gets picked on more because of how he acts. He's different—that whole living in his own bubble thing and not seeming to care what other people think. It probably drives the so-called bullies nuts that they can't get to him.

I wish I had a bubble. Maybe if I hang around Kal enough, I can figure out how to hide inside of his with him.

If we don't get out of the forest I won't have to worry about it anymore. We'll just turn into monkeys and live in the trees.

I wonder if there're such things as monkey bullies?

TWENTY

"So?" Kal has been sitting very still for a very long time. I'm starting to think he fell asleep with his eyes open.

"Pardon?" He looks at me as if he's surprised I'm still here.

"So, have you figured out what we should do yet? We have to get back to civilization soon, or we'll both be missing."

"I know. It's just that if we go in the wrong direction we could really become lost. This forest is huge. I can't remember exactly how many acres, but I think it's big enough that you could disappear for days or weeks even."

"Okay. That's all good information, but it doesn't really help much. What's the plan?"

"We head toward the sun and hope that there is a road in that direction." He nods as if he's said something smart.

"I was already doing that when you found me! We're just going to end up right back where we started."

"I don't think so. I think we'll end up somewhere useful. It's around lunchtime, so if we're facing the sun, we're heading west. I know that much about navigating."

"Yeah, well, how do you know that heading west will get us somewhere useful? Maybe east is better." After all, it seems that I've been heading east all morning. Awesome.

"We have to have some kind of plan and I think my house is west of here, although I'm not one hundred percent sure. I'm about sixty percent sure. I think. Maybe. Anyway, more than fifty, which makes it a viable plan."

"Thanks for the math lesson." I smile at him, but he looks at me in total panic.

"I missed my math class! We were supposed to have a geometry test today. I've never missed a test before. What happens when you miss a test?"

"You're sixteen and never missed a math test? Don't you ever get sick?"

"Not really. I avoid germs."

"Right. Of course you do. Well, don't worry. They usually just let you do a makeup test another day. No big deal."

He looks at me and nods. His eyes tell me it's a really big deal to him.

"They will have noticed my absence by now. They'll call my mother."

"Yeah. Computer attendance lady. But it's cool. You'll be home before your mom gets there. You can just erase the message and write your own note for tomorrow—or so

I've heard." I try grinning at him but he doesn't notice. He's still upset about missing his test. I'm more worried about geography than geometry. I should say that out loud and try to get a laugh out of him.

"Erasing the message and forging a note. More lies. I don't know if I can tell any more lies." He doesn't sound like anything would make him laugh right now.

"You don't really have to. When we get out of here, I'll go home and fix everything, and you can tell your mom whatever you need to. I promise."

I hope I can keep my promise. I owe him that.

"All right. I guess we have to start walking. Follow me."

He heads off through the trees, pushing branches away from his face and forgetting about me, letting them swing back so that I have to constantly fling my arms around so I don't lose an eye. I don't complain to him though. He's obviously a man on a mission, and if I distract him, he'll likely forget what he's doing.

We walk and walk for what seems like hours. Kal never says a word, and the silence is starting to get to me.

"So, I went on one of those charity marathon walks once with Celina. We walked for about three hours and I thought I was going to pass out. I seriously think you and I have been going at least that long or even longer, and I can't believe I'm still moving. The stupid sun is just laughing at us, watching us sweat to death while we try to figure out if west is best. Everything looks the same no matter where we go, and I'm pretty sure we're just going around in circles."

"You need to stop talking and conserve your energy."

"So, in other words, shut up?"

Kal ignores me and just keeps walking. Suddenly he stops and points dead ahead.

"Look!" He sounds excited. I try to figure out what he's so happy about but I don't see anything except more trees.

"At what?"

"There's a hill. See? Over to the left. The trees start sloping upwards. If we climb up there, we can get a good look at where we are and maybe figure out where we should be going."

"I thought you already knew where we should be going!"

"I don't *know*. I'm just making an educated guess."

"And now you want us to climb up a big hill so we can see if your guess is right or not?"

"Yes. It can be like an experiment. I like experiments."

"Why am I not surprised?"

"I don't know." He answers my non-question and heads left without looking at me.

"Wait for me!" I raise my voice as he speeds up almost out of sight. He stops to let me catch up.

"Why did you want me to wait?" he asks, looking impatient.

"Because it isn't polite to run ahead like that. I don't really want to be lost on my own." Social skills lessons in the woods.

"I thought it was polite to get there before you, so you didn't have to come all the way up. I am in exponentially better shape than you, and it is easier for me to get to the top."

"*Exponentially* better shape? Seriously?" I'm not even sure what that means.

"Very seriously. I am smaller and faster than you. I like exponents."

"You like exponents. That's nice." *Why the hell are we talking about math again?*

"One number multiplying itself over and over, independent from all of the other numbers but making more and more of them at the same time. I wish I could multiply myself so that I could spread out and cover more ground."

"*What* are you talking about?"

"Getting to the top, of course." He looks at me as if I have very little in the brains department and then takes off without waiting for me. Again.

We start climbing. The hill is a lot steeper than it looked from a distance. My legs start screaming at me to sit down, but Kal is just bouncing along ahead of me like he's done this a thousand times. He's pretty agile for a kid who lives inside of his computer most of the time. Must be all those exponents he likes so much.

When I was really little, I wanted to be a dancer. I even went to lessons for a while before we started moving so much. I remember my ballet teacher always trying to get us to stretch our pudgy little arms gracefully above our heads so we formed a perfect line from toes to finger tips. She would walk around with the little stick she used to tap in time to the music and use it to draw an imaginary line up the side of our not very straight bodies. I was always a little afraid that she was going to whack me on the head with it because I could never seem to get my legs and arms to cooperate. She would call out "Stretch up, my little dancers. Reach your fingers up to the light." And I would close my eyes and reach with all my might, imagining that I was outside and reaching for the sun like a giant ballet queen, who could do anything she wanted to do, even if her feet weren't turned out in perfect first position. I had everything I loved best in that moment—dancing and sunshine. All I needed was a unicorn to come prancing by, and life would have been perfect.

I do *not* love sunshine today. It's too hot and it is not helping us get anywhere useful.

I wish I could do some ballet leaps now so I could get up this hill faster. I am seriously, completely, and totally out of shape in every possible way. I'm panting so much I sound like a train going by. I think Kal has forgotten I'm back here again. This is so not fun.

I can't be a baby about this. I have to force myself to catch up to him and help get us out of here. I can do this. I take a deep breath and force my legs into a jogging motion. Everything on my body starts to jiggle uncomfortably, but I keep going because I am a true hero.

After about six seconds I stop and bend over double, hands on knees, sweating and panting. Jogging sucks. Seriously.

I look up to see where Kal is, but he's out of my sight. Nice. He's actually forgotten that I'm here, and he's supposed to be leading me to safety. Such a gentleman. Shaking my head, I try to get my breathing under control so that I can keep climbing. After a few more minutes, I can see the top but still no Kal.

I hear a crashing sound over to my left. It must be him. I guess he doubled back to get me. Such a nice guy.

"So, you're back." I start talking before I see him. Turning around I find myself looking into a pair of very dark, very brown, and very horrified eyes. Not Kal's eyes. A poor deer that thinks I'm some kind of new predator let loose in her forest. She stands completely still, hoping I won't notice her. Not a very good self-defence system. Kind of explains how hunters manage to kill so many.

"It's all right, I won't hurt you," I tell her, assuming that somehow the sound of a human voice will be comforting. The deer lets out a very strange sound, like an out of tune trumpet, and literally turns tail and runs away from me. Two steps behind her is the cutest little fawn I've ever seen, outside of a Bambi movie. They run gracefully through the forest, managing to leap over bushes and dodge under branches like some kind of Olympic gymnastics team.

So awesome. I wish I was a deer, except for the whole getting shot by people and eaten by wolves part.

And now I'm even farther behind, and Kal still hasn't noticed that I'm missing, which is a bit funny when you think about it because my being missing is why we're here in the first place.

Taking the time to watch the deer has let me catch my breath so that I can pick up the pace a bit. I hike my sore legs up the rest of the hill, preparing my speech about how friends don't disappear on friends, so that I have it ready when I finally find Kal. I might not be the big expert on friendship that I used to pretend to be, but I still know that taking off on someone when you're both lost in the woods is just plain rude.

I finally creep my way to the top of the hill and I stand there, looking around. I'm surprised to see that the land drops down into what looks almost like a cliff on the other side. Glad we didn't try to climb up that! I can see really far from up here. Trees, trees, and more trees. Not a road in sight.

Not a Kal in sight.

"Kal! Where the hell are you?" I yell it as loudly as my lungs will let me. I'm pretty sure they're deflated by now. I stand still and listen. I can hear birds yelling at each other and animals moving through the trees. I hope they're all deer and bunnies and nothing more exciting. I mean, I think wolves are interesting, but I still don't want to meet one up front and personal.

"Kal! Where are you? I can't see you!" I'm screaming by now, upsetting the ecosystem by scaring all the animals.

I need some binoculars. Where is he? Did he go all the way home without me?

"Kal! Frederick!! Where are you?!" Upping the ante by using his real, three-syllable name. I peer down the steep side of the hill, trying to figure out which way he went. About half-way down, I see something, like a bag or a coat or—I don't know what it is exactly, but it's something that just doesn't fit. *One of these things is not like the others.* Sesame Street flashback.

I start down, slipping and sliding my way and grabbing at anything to try to slow myself down. After a few seconds,

I figure out what I should have realized right away.

It's not a bag or a coat.

It's Kal.

And he isn't moving.

TWENTY-ONE

Shit, shit, shit, shit, shit, shit—I can't slow myself down! I have to get to him without falling and landing on him. He has to be okay. He *has* to be.

"Kal!" I yell his name as I skid down the last few feet. He's lying on his side with his head against a rock. There's blood on his forehead and on the rock. My stomach starts to heave.

Stop it! This is no time for puking. I have to help him.

I take several deep breaths, fighting for control so that I can figure out what's going on with him.

"Kal? Can you hear me?" Nothing. I reach over to touch his neck to see if he has a pulse but my hands are shaking, and I can't feel him properly. I lean forward to try to see if his chest is going up and down but the rest of me is trembling so badly that I can't tell if he's moving, or if it's just me.

I don't know what to do! Kal's the one who knows everything.

"Kal. You have to wake up. I don't know what to do!" I push his shoulder as if somehow that's going to fix everything. His head is bleeding. I need to make it stop doing that.

I look around, trying to figure out what I'm supposed to use. There's nothing. I look down at my feet. My socks are probably seriously gross by now, but I can't think of anything else, so I take one off. I turn it inside out, hoping that there's less dirt on the inside. Rolling it up, I press it to the cut on his head.

I can't see how bad it is because there's so much blood. Heads bleed a lot, but that doesn't always mean that the person is hurt really badly. When I was three, I was skipping up our front walkway and tripped over my own big feet. I didn't fall hard, just kind of slumped down on my knees, but my forehead made friends with the cement step and suddenly everything looked red. I remember my mother screaming and picking me up, and then something wet was pressed against my head. Dad took us to the hospital and a nice doctor sewed my head up with big black stitches. People stared at me for a while after that...I looked like some kind of weird doll made by a mad scientist or something. My mother made me get bangs after the stitches came out. I still have the scar.

Maybe Kal just needs a couple of stitches and some bangs. Except that he passed out and I didn't. I stayed awake and cried a lot.

I keep pressing the sock to his head. When he does

wake up, he's going to be seriously upset that there's a dirty sock making contact with his bodily fluids. The thought makes me laugh and cry at the same time.

I put my other hand on his chest and this time I'm pretty sure I can feel it going up and down. I hope it's not just wishful thinking. I know how to do CPR because we learned it in school, but I'm pretty sure Kal would rather die than make mouth-to-mouth contact with another human being. He's the biggest germaphobe I know.

I don't know how long he's been lying here like this. I didn't hear him fall. Was it before I saw the deer or after? Has it been five minutes or fifteen? Does it matter?

I sit there with my bloody sock on his head and my dirty hand on his chest for what seems like hours but is probably only minutes. I can't tell. My mother always says "Time flies when you're having fun," so I guess the opposite is true. Time crawls when life sucks.

My mother would know what to do if she was here. She thinks she knows everything, which bugs the crap out of me because she's so often right. At least about things like this. There's no way she would ever be out in the woods without a complete first aid kit in one hand and some sort of magic bag in the other hand that would give us food and water. We have nothing to eat or drink and no way to fix Kal's head.

I'm scared to take the sock away and see how bad the cut is. He probably needs stitches. I don't know what happens if you don't get them when you need them. Will he just keep on bleeding until he's dried out and gone? I press harder.

"Ow!" Kal's eyes are still closed. He reaches one hand

up toward his head and then just drops it down again as if it's too heavy to lift.

"Kal! Are you okay?" Stupid question. He's lying in the dirt with my sock stuck to his bloody head.

"I don't think so. My head hurts."

"Yeah, I know. You have a cut." He starts to reach up again.

"It's all right. I have something on it to stop the bleeding." I press his arm back down gently.

"Bleeding! I'm bleeding?!" His eyes fly open, and he looks at me, totally freaked out.

"Not so much now. It's going to be okay. We just have to get home and get you fixed up." Now I sound like my mother.

"I don't like to bleed. My blood belongs inside of me. I need it."

"You have lots more where that came from. I've bled lots of times and I'm still fine." Now *that* should make him feel better.

"I'm not you. I don't like to bleed."

"Nobody likes to bleed."

"We have to get home. My mother will know what to do." His voice is shaky, and I think he's going to cry.

"We are going to get home as soon as I figure out how. But you have to try to calm down, or you're going to make your head feel worse. Try to relax a bit."

"Relax? I can't relax when I have a cut on my head and I don't know where I am! I feel like an energy drink!"

"What?" He's thirsty?

"An energy drink. I bought one once and drank some,

and my heart started racing. I never understood what that expression meant before, but then I drank the drink and felt like I do now. My heart is trying to outrun my brain. Which just hit a rock. Which is making me bleed!" He starts to breathe really fast and is shifting around as if he's trying to get up. I try to hold him still, but even in his condition he can't stand to be touched, so he's brushing me away like he thinks I'm a blood-sucking parasite. My heart's joining the race and pounding like crazy as I start to panic along with him.

"Kal. If you move around too much, your head will start to bleed faster. If you want it to stop, you have to keep your body still." I don't even know if that's true or not, but I say it in this teacher voice so that it sounds true, hoping that it will make him believe it. Teachers make everything sound true, even though they probably have no idea what they're talking about half the time.

"You're probably right. I'll try." He looks at me, his eyes big and trusting like he's a little kid, and I'm an adult who will take care of him.

"Listen, Kal. I need to leave you for just a few minutes. I want to see if I can figure out where we are and maybe see if there's any water anywhere."

"There's water in the knapsack. And some granola bars. And wet wipes. I put them there for you yesterday."

"My knapsack? I thought I left that at your place."

"You did, but I brought it when I came looking for you. Didn't you notice?"

"No." Figures he'd remember that. Even with his head split open, he's more with it than I am right now.

"I think I dropped it when I fell though."

"I'll find it, clean you up a bit, and then we'll figure out what to do next. Okay?"

"I'm tired, and my head hurts." His voice is so sad and small that it makes my stomach hurt.

"Just rest, and I'll be back soon."

He closes his eyes and I touch him gently on the top of the head. He raises his hand to brush me away like an irritating fly. It makes me both smile and start to cry again as I head back up the hillside to find the knapsack.

Maybe I'll run into a brilliant how-to-escape-the-woods idea while I'm at it.

TWENTY-TWO

I start moving up the hill, which is so impossibly straight that it feels more like a cliff. I'm slipping and sliding with every step. What is that other Mom expression? One step forward and two steps back. I always just thought it meant I suck at school, but now I know what it really means.

I grab at whatever random branches I can find to break my own fall. All we would need now is for me to actually slip all the way down and land on Kal's sore head. That would kill him for sure. My running shoes have no tread on them at all, and it's taking forever to move forward.

After a while I see something blue over to the side. Unless someone else is wandering around here getting lost, my guess is that I'm looking at my knapsack. It must have really flown from Kal when he fell, because it's pretty far away. I have to get it, though, so I need to figure out how to move across the hill instead of up. Great.

Slowly seems to be my only choice. I'm leaning so far forward that I'm almost lying down, as I sidestep my way across the rough ground. Every bit of me is covered in sweat and I imagine I smell like the boys' locker room. I went in there once on a dare at my last school. It was not pleasant.

I finally get to the bag and try to keep my balance as I grab it and fling it over my shoulder. I try to glance down to see what Kal is doing, but that almost makes me lose my balance, so I look up instead. The top still looks far away I need to try to see where we are, but I need to get him cleaned up before he gets an infection or something else just as horrible. I don't know if I should keep heading up, or go back down and try to fix Kal.

It's actually a no brainer. There is no choice here.

Going down is faster but scarier than going up. I head straight down from where I found the bag, so that I don't have to worry about falling on Kal. When I get down to his level, the ground isn't as steep, and it's relatively easy to move across to where he's still lying.

"I found it. Are you okay?"

"No. I am not. I already told you that." He opens his eyes and looks at me. I'm glad he can't see himself. He looks terrible. His hair is full of dirt and leaves, and my dirty sock is glued to his forehead.

"I need to try to clean your forehead a little and it's going to hurt."

"I don't like pain."

"No one much does. I still have to do it, and you have to try to relax."

"This is not a very relaxing situation." His voice is so serious that it makes me laugh for a second.

"This isn't funny!" He looks as offended as he sounds. Which is fair, seeing as he's right. It is *so* not funny.

"I know. I'm sorry. Just nerves."

"You're nervous about cleaning me? That doesn't sound very positive."

"No, I didn't mean that." *Yes I did.* "I just meant that the whole situation is a bit hard on my nerves. I'm cool with the cleaning." I add a smile to soften the lie, grabbing the bag and opening it. There are two bottles of water in there, along with a little pack of those wet wipe things that mothers use on little kids. I take one bottle and the pack out and set them on a rock near Kal's head.

"I have to move the so—cloth from your head and it's going to pull a little." I almost said sock. If he knew that's what I used to stop the bleeding he'd pass right out again.

"I'll be brave."

"I know. You can just imagine you're one of those X-Men guys or whatever. They're all brave, right?"

"I'm too old for that kind of game. I'll just imagine that *I'm* brave."

"Whatever works. Just try to lie still, and I'll try to be gentle and fast."

I'm really scared to do this. What if taking the sock off rips his head open again and he starts bleeding even more? But if I don't take it off, he could get an infection and that could even be worse than bleeding. I think. I don't know!

I take a deep breath and try to stop my hands from

trembling. I carefully start to peel the sock away from his head. It sticks, and I know it's got to be killing him but he never makes a sound. I get it off and the cut doesn't seem to be bleeding too much, just kind of oozing around the edges. I can't tell how deep it is, but I don't really want to know. I can't do anything about it one way or the other.

I throw the sock as far away as I can so that Kal won't see it.

"Close your eyes so I don't get water in them," I say to him, as I take the water bottle and uncap it. I pour some gently onto his forehead to wash off some of the mess, and then I take a wet wipe and start to clean. Kal winces a little as I remove some crusty mess from the cut but he stays silent.

I don't have a bandage to put across his head. I need to find something to protect him. I dig through the bag but there's nothing. I look at Kal and notice he's wearing a belt made out of some kind of elastic material. That'll do.

"Kal I need your belt."

"What?" His eyes fly open and both hands move to protect his waist.

"I just need something to wrap around your head to keep something on your cut so it stays clean. I can't find anything else. You can take it off yourself. I promise I won't touch."

He looks at me for a second and then unhooks the belt, pulling it through the loops of his pants. The effort seems to be hurting him, but I know he doesn't want my help. Too much personal space invasion.

I take a few of the wipes and fold them together to make a sort of bandage. I use one to clean off his belt and then wrap it around his head, tying it at the back. He looks like a pirate, who has his patch up too high.

"There. That's the best I can do for now. You should try to drink some of the leftover water."

"I can't drink lying down. I have to try to sit up." He shifts his weight a little and tries rolling to the side.

"I'm so dizzy. I can't get up!"

"It's okay. I'll help you drink."

"You keep saying it's okay, but it really isn't. Okay doesn't mean anything, you know. Especially not now. Just empty syllables."

"Sorry. I'll try to stop saying it. I have to put my arm behind your head to help you move up a bit so you can drink. Are you o—all right with that?"

"Not really, but I suppose there is no choice."

I put my left arm behind his head and push it up a little while I tilt the water bottle to his lips with my right. He takes a couple of mouthfuls and then shakes his head, which makes him wince again.

"We have to conserve water. Only a bit at a time. I know that much about being lost."

"I figured that part out also. I actually used to camp sometimes when I was younger. My dad and I got sort of lost once. I have a bit of an idea of what it's like." That's a big fat lie. Being lost with your father is a completely different experience. He carried me around on his shoulders and sang silly songs so I wouldn't be scared. Somehow, I don't think Kal would appreciate that method. I put the water back in the bag. I'm getting hungry.

"Do you want a granola bar?"

"No, my stomach is not very happy right now. Maybe later," he says in that sad little voice that makes my stomach feel sick also. I guess we'll both have one later.

He drifts off, hopefully just to sleep. I check his diver's watch to make sure it's working. I can't let him sleep more than an hour at a time. I remember my mother telling the story of my head cut, and she always talked about how hard it was to keep waking me up all night long and how she was afraid to go to sleep herself in case I didn't wake up. Now I know how she felt.

It's after six o'clock. I can't believe it's so late. Even though it felt like we were walking for hours, some part of me didn't believe it was true. If I wasn't so totally pissed off at myself, I'd feel a little proud that I could actually keep moving that long.

I sit down to rest for a few minutes before trying to climb back up to the top and see if I can figure out which way we should go, once Kal can move again. I stare at him, watching closely to make sure that his chest is still moving up and down.

I can't believe we're here. That I made us both be here. Kal was just minding his own business when I got in his face that day we met in the library. When I first walked in I saw him sitting there, hiding way back in the corner, giving out a very strong keep-away vibe. So, of course, I walked right up to him and started reading over his shoulder. He was so pissed when he noticed me that I thought he was going smack me in the face with his phone. He was such a weird little guy that it didn't occur to me, at first, that we could turn into actual friends.

I don't even know how it happened. Maybe it's because we're both Reject Roomers. Whatever it is, we turned into friends, whether he wants to admit it or not.

I'm the one who pushed the friendship. I kept telling him that I'm the big expert on friends and that he should listen to me. He kept telling me that he was used to being on his own, that he didn't mind being friendless and didn't really have any need for one. But I wore him down.

And now I seem to have *brought* him down.

TWENTY-THREE

"Kal. Wake up!"

"I'm not sleeping. Just resting my eyes." He opens them and looks at me. "Did you see anything from the top?"

"I haven't made it back up there. I didn't see anything the first time, but I didn't really take enough time to look. It's getting dark, so I think we're going to have to wait until morning to really see what's going on."

"Morning? You think we have to stay here until morning? How can we do that?" He starts to sit up and then remembers his head and lies back down.

"I think we have to. You can't exactly jog out of here right now and I'm not leaving without you. We'll be all right here. I'm going to stay awake and keep watch so you can sleep when you need to."

"Keep watch for what?"

"Just for whatever might find us interesting I guess."

"What are you talking about? I don't think most animals find humans very interesting. They mostly find us to be violent. People seem to mostly want to shoot them or cut down their trees. Do you think they are interested in taking revenge on the human race by eating us?"

"Whoa! Slow down! I didn't mean anything like that. Nothing in here wants to eat us." *I hope.* "Anyway, speaking of eating, it's been a long time since either of us ate anything. We should at least split a granola bar and then save one for the morning." I try a quick subject change so I don't panic him any more than he already is.

"All right. I guess."

"First, let's try to get you sitting a little." He nods slightly and we very gently manage to shift him into a halfway sitting position without his head exploding. Progress.

I pull a granola bar out of the bag. It's the kind of packet that has the two bars in it, which makes splitting it easy. I should really give him more than half because he's less than half my size and doesn't have as much of his own body to live off, if we're stuck here for a while.

"Here. You have this one and half of mine." I hand him the food, feeling very noble.

"No. We split it evenly. It's the only fair way."

"I'm bigger than you are. I don't need it as much."

"It could be just the opposite. Maybe you have to work harder because you're bigger so you need it more. It doesn't matter. We're sharing equally. It would feel inappropriate to do it your way."

"Right. Of course, you could say something like *You're not bigger than me, you're just a delicate little girl.*"

"Why would I say that? It's not true." He looks so confused that I have to laugh.

"I can always count on you for a straight answer. At least you don't play all those games most people do."

"Games?"

"Most people tell a lot of little lies, trying to either protect or hurt your feelings, depending on who they are."

"I've been telling a lot of lies recently."

"That's my fault, not yours. We'll get out of here by morning and I'll fix everything and you won't have to tell any more lies for me. I'm sure that the searchers would look in these woods, seeing as you live right in front of them and your mom knows you like to hang out on your tree rock."

Kal swallows a bit of granola. "The searchers?"

"The people who are looking for us." Now *I'm* defining words?

"I know what searchers are. The fact that you seem to think that they'd be looking for me already rather discredits your twenty-four-hour theory."

"Yeah, well I think my parents already proved me wrong on that one. I guess the rules are different for kids, even at my age. Your mom wouldn't have waited very long before calling the cops. They'll already be calling people and looking around the neighborhood. I don't think they'd do much searching in the woods at night, but I'm sure they'll be here by morning." I'm not sure of anything but I can't tell him that.

"How will they find us?"

"I guess we try to start moving again and make a lot of noise. We'll scare off the deer, but hopefully attract some attention at the same time."

"That's actually a good idea!" He sounds so surprised that I can't help but laugh.

"Thanks for sounding so shocked that I could have a good idea."

"I'm not shocked that you had it. I'm just surprised that I didn't think of it first."

"Oh, well that's so much better, then."

"That's good."

I don't know why I bother with sarcasm with Kal. It floats right over his bubble and disappears.

"I think I should lie down again," Kal says, looking a little green.

"Oh, sure. Here try this under your head." I bunch up the knapsack to make the closest thing to a pillow that I can. We ease him down until he's lying flat again. He closes his eyes.

"So, do you want to try to sleep?"

"No. I can't sleep right now. It's still a bit light out and I only sleep in the dark, which at home is friendly, but I don't think it will be so friendly here. I've never slept outside before."

"I have, with my dad. It's not so bad. It would be better if we had sleeping bags though." It would be even better if we had my dad.

"I'm going to keep my eyes closed, but you can talk to me if you want."

He's actually asking me to talk to him? He's always telling

me that he thinks I use too many words—his way of trying to shut me up. He's either really scared or he hit his head harder than I thought. So, now I have to think of something to talk about that won't make him even more scared, or give him a bigger headache.

Maybe I should talk to him about that night with Eric and Peter and why I really went away. It's not like we have much else to do out here. Maybe if I hear myself talk about it out loud, I can decide what I'm going to tell my parents—if I ever see them again.

But maybe if I tell him, he'll think I'm stupid or gross or slutty or something. Does he even know what *slutty* means? He gets all embarrassed every time I try to talk to him about sex. It's kind of why I keep doing it. He looks cute all red faced and flustered.

This isn't a cute conversation to have, though. If he gets embarrassed or grossed out, there's nowhere for either of us to go.

"You aren't talking," he says. Does he actually sound disappointed, or am I imagining things? He's going to be really disappointed in a minute.

I have to tell someone or I'm going to lose what's left of my mind.

I'm going to do it.

"Angel? Did you fall asleep?" Kal sounds panicky again.

"No, no. Sorry. I was just thinking."

"About what?"

"About the real reason I had to get away."

"I thought the reason was how mean everyone was

being to you at our school. I never thought that was a very good reason for leaving, by the way."

"No?"

"No. It's been my experience that there are always mean people around. Running away from them works well when they're trying to kick you, but if all they're using is words, it's best just to put your shields up."

"Shields? Like knights in shining armor use?" Could have used one of those that night. Actually it would have been useful to have the whole shiny suit. And maybe a nice sharp sword to go with it.

"Sort of, only these ones are invisible. You can use them to keep things out of your insides, like staring eyes and ugly words. No one can get to you if you have your shields up."

"Sounds like something I could use. Where do you buy them?" He opens his eyes and looks at me in complete seriousness. Jokes float past him the same way as sarcasm does most of the time. *My* jokes, anyway.

"Shields aren't for sale. You have to create them with your mind. I didn't have any when I was a little boy, and it hurt to have people try to get inside of me through my eyes. Everyone was always telling me to look at them, make eye contact. I don't even know why. I had to learn how to make it look like they were getting in, when really I had my defences up so that they couldn't."

"Can you teach me how to do that?"

"I don't know. No one's ever asked me that before. I'd have to think about it."

"That's cool. I'm not going anywhere."

"Until tomorrow. Right?" He sounds like a little kid who's afraid that Santa Claus isn't coming.

"Right. Tomorrow we're going home."

"Tonight we're sleeping outside, which does not feel natural to me. Which is odd because sleeping outside in nature should feel natural."

"Kal, did you just make a joke?" I start to laugh but he doesn't even crack a smile. He just stares at me with his usual Angel-is-nuts expression.

"Not that I'm aware of," he says totally seriously, which somehow just makes me want to laugh more, but I choke it back because he's still staring at me. I cough a few times, instead. Once I finally shut up, he closes his eyes.

"So, do you want to sleep now?" I'm a little disappointed, but relieved at the same time that I don't have to tell him my sad little story.

"No, not yet. You said you were going to tell me something. I want to listen."

Oh. Okay then. So much for relieved.

I take a deep breath and nod my head, even though he isn't looking at me.

I guess it's time.

TWENTY-FOUR

Kal listens silently while I tell him what I remember about what happened that Friday night. The words come out of me in bits and pieces, the same way the memories do, and I'm not even sure if I'm making any sense.

"I'm so scared and screwed up. It's making me crazy inside my head every time I think about it. And it just makes it so much worse that I know it was my fault because I had too much to drink and must have led Eric on somehow. It scares me to think that I don't remember what actually happened. I don't know what Peter was doing there. I don't know what Peter *did* there. Did he do anything to me? I don't even know for sure what Eric actually did, what *I* did or how far we went before I came to my senses a little. The one thing I do know is that I'm afraid to go back to school again. Four days of hell waiting for Peter to show someone a picture or video of me making a total fool of myself. Just waiting until I felt like I was going out of my mind and starting to think that having it actually happen would be better than this horrible feeling of wondering if it would. I had to get away before I completely lost my mind. So I made up a story about not being able to handle the bullying anymore and created my big plan that didn't end up working."

"The plan you told me that I couldn't tell anyone else."

"Yeah, that didn't work out very well for anyone, did it?"

"Especially not for me."

"I bet Peter's done it by now. After all, I'm famous with my picture on the news. I'll bet Peter is having a great time showing everyone his pictures—or video—of the missing idiot. Eric's probably telling everyone how easy I am when I have a few drinks in me, and what a lightweight I am booze wise. Finally, I'm a lightweight. I think it would be best for everyone if I just stay missing forever."

"It wouldn't be best for me. If you stay missing , so do I."

"Good point. I got so wrapped up in telling you my pathetic story that I forgot where I was for a moment."

"You're in the woods. The very dark woods."

"Thanks for the update."

"Why didn't you tell your parents about it? Maybe they would have helped you figure things out and you wouldn't have had to go missing."

"I can't tell my mother the truth. She would kill me. She's been pounding the 'evils of alcohol' speech into my brain since I was about ten years old. She's told me over and over again how dangerous it is for kids to drink too much. How it reduces inhibitions so girls find themselves in what she calls compromising situations and how some boys can take advantage of that, maybe because their inhibitions are missing, too, or just because they're assholes. My mother didn't say that last part. I added that. I can't tell her that I did the one thing she's begged me a thousand times not to. I'd never get out of the house again. If I ever get back into it, that is."

"What about your father?"

"I can't tell him either because he'd probably want to go and kick the shit out of both guys. God, this is all such a mess! When I woke up Saturday, I was so sick I felt like I wanted to curl up and sleep for a week. And then when I started to remember what happened, I wanted to curl up and die."

"Why?"

"Why what?" *Why am I an idiot?*

"Why did you want to die?"

"I didn't actually want to *die*. I don't think. I just felt like I never wanted to show my face anywhere ever again."

"Why?"

"Why do you think?" Does he actually not get it?

"I don't know. That's why I asked."

"Peter Murphy was standing there with his phone out. He was probably taking pictures or even a video to post online." The thought makes me want to puke up my granola bar. I've read those stories about girls who get their picture put online, and then their reputation is completely ruined, and everyone hates them. It's not even that I have much of a reputation to ruin, but I don't want one created for me by Peter and Eric, either.

"Why would he want to do that?"

"Just to be an asshole. To be horrible and mean and show off what big men they are because they got me drunk and took me somewhere to make out with me when I was so out of it I didn't even know what I was doing!"

"They *got* you drunk? How did they make you drink the beer?" He sounds curious.

"What? No. No one made me drink it. Not exactly. I mean, I guess I drank it because Eric told me to try it and said I looked cute doing it." That sounds so lame when I say it out loud.

"I didn't know drinking alcohol was cute. I've never tried it. I like control. I've read that it takes that away."

"Now you sound like my mom. Who was right. Again. Which pisses me off so much. I really don't want to have to tell her about this."

"Do you have to?"

"I don't know. I have to give her some reason to explain why I left. I would have to tell her the truth if those pictures have made it to the Internet. She'll find out from someone in this backward mini-town."

"Are you sure Peter took pictures?" I look at him for a second, confused. Of course, Peter took pictures. He had his phone out, right?

"I guess I'm not *sure*. I just assumed."

"I don't really understand why he would take pictures, but I don't understand assholes or mean people." He smiles when he says assholes.

"You like the word *assholes* do you? I never hear you

swear much." Changing the subject. Taking a break.

"I like to swear inside of my head sometimes. Swear words are very expressive. My mother doesn't like to hear them though, so I'm careful to keep them inside. I got in trouble once."

"Oh, really?" This should be good. Divert the attention away from my mess for a few minutes.

"When I was in grade six, I had an educational assistant, Mrs. Greenough, who was supposed to be helping me with my social skills. She decided that one of the things that would help me the most would be to understand my *disorder.*" The way he says *disorder* makes it clear that he *can* understand sarcasm when he wants to. He takes a deep breath and keeps going.

"I found it silly and demeaning, but I knew that school staff didn't really like to be told that sort of thing, so I kept it to myself. She explained who Asperger was and why he invented a disorder and why I was considered a good candidate for the label. Then she gave me a marker and asked me to draw how I felt about what she had said. To draw my understanding of Asperger's Syndrome."

"That must have been fun."

"Actually it was. I drew a hamburger bun with two bum cheeks in it. An Ass Burger."

I start to laugh. He looks at me totally seriously but there's this little glint in his eyes that makes me laugh so hard that my stomach starts to hurt, and tears start pouring down my cheeks.

"Oh, my God. I love that! That is the best story ever! You

are awesome!" I can't believe he did that! Kal actually has a sense of humor hiding in there somewhere. Too bad I ruined my life. It might have been fun to get to know him better.

"Mrs. Greenough didn't think so. My mother, either. She took my computer away for a week. So I don't use bad language out loud, and I usually keep jokes to myself. Why do you think Peter is such an asshole that he would take pictures?"

Peter's name makes me stop laughing. My stomach keeps hurting and the tears keep pouring though.

"I don't know. He just is. I've read about people taking that kind of picture and then posting it to humiliate other people. I just…assumed Peter was doing that. You call Peter a Despiser because he's so mean to everyone."

"Yes, but I find that most Despisers do their best not to get caught. Sometimes they aren't smart enough to avoid it, but Peter seems like the type to keep away from people who will discipline him. Posting pictures doesn't seem a very good way to hide."

"Maybe that's why I didn't see or hear anything." I say it mostly to myself, but Kal hears me.

"That would make sense."

"They could still have told people about it. And the other kids at the party could have seen me leave with them. This is still a totally embarrassing mess and all my fault."

"Why?" Again with the *why*. This is worse than being questioned by my mother.

"Why *what*?" Trying to keep my voice from sounding pissed. I know he really doesn't understand this kind of thing.

I'll bet he's never been to a party in his life.

"Why is it all your fault?"

"I went to a party that I didn't really belong at. I drank the beer. I went with them. I obviously gave them the idea that I wanted to fool around."

"By fool around you mean that you gave them the idea you wanted to have Eric lie on top of you and put his hand under your shirt while Peter watched?" He isn't judging. He's really just trying to figure it out.

"No! I can't have done that! I wouldn't have done that. Even drunk. I don't think. But that's the problem. I really don't know! I hate this feeling! I want to remember. I feel like I left pieces of myself behind at that stupid party that I'll never find again."

"I can't imagine what that feels like. Not knowing. They were drinking also?"

"Yes."

"As much as you?"

"I don't know. Maybe. I know I saw Eric have some beer but, I actually have no idea how much."

"Why were there two?"

"Two?"

"Two boys and only one of you. Is that what usually happens when a boy thinks a girl wants to…fool around? It sounds unbalanced to me. I thought it was usually one and one."

He's right, of course. It isn't usually a threesome. I wouldn't have agreed to that even if I drank a whole case of beer. Right?

"Usually."

"So, they knew you were drunk and they knew it should be one and one but took you away with them, anyway. It doesn't sound right to me." He shakes his head then stops and puts his hand up to the fake bandage for a second. His head must really hurt, but he isn't complaining.

"No, it wasn't."

"Eric left you alone when you told him to."

"Yes. Thank God."

"Left you alone in the dark after taking you out there with them in the first place! Anyone should know that's wrong. Even an asshole." Kal sounds angry. I don't think I've ever heard him sound angry before.

"Yeah, well, lots of things were wrong about that night." I rub my forehead. Maybe if I do it hard enough I can erase the whole thing. The memory.

"Maybe they don't want to publicize all of the things they did wrong."

I never thought about it like that before. Could he be right? Could they be feeling scared that they'll get in trouble if anyone finds out?

If he's right, does that mean it's over?

"So, maybe they just want to forget it. They're probably happy I'm missing so they can pretend it never happened."

"Is that a good thing?"

"Sure. I'd like to pretend it never happened. If I thought they were going to do that, I'd try to figure out something else to tell my parents so I can forget about it too."

Kal is quiet for a long time, so long that I think he's

fallen asleep. I'm just about to check and see when he starts talking again.

"I guess I don't know a lot about social situations. I don't even know if this *is* a social situation. But if everyone just pretends it didn't happen, it might happen again because everyone would be pretending no one got hurt. Would that be all right?"

If my mother said any of that to me, I'd think she was lecturing. When Kal says it, it just sounds like he's trying to work out some kind of math problem and it kind of makes sense.

I'd like to pretend it never happened. I'd still never let it happen again. I learned my lesson, which would make my mother extremely happy.

But if *they* are allowed to pretend it never happened, will they understand that what they did was wrong? Or will they do it again with someone else?

Is it my job to tell, so they don't?

TWENTY-FIVE

Kal seems to be worn out from all of our talking, and I think he's actually fallen asleep. I check his watch as carefully as I can so I don't wake him up. I should have taken it off when he was awake so I can keep checking it every few minutes. I think his head has stopped bleeding. I hope it's not getting infected under that sad excuse for a bandage. I sit looking at him in the dim moonlight. I'm very happy that it's a clear night. The sky is much friendlier when the moon and stars are out.

When I was little, I thought that stars were crystal fairies twinkling their way home at night. It was a big letdown when I found out the truth in science class.

There weren't any stars the night that Eric and Peter left me alone in a strange field. It was completely dark and extremely scary. I was still drunk and dizzy. I was upset and confused by what happened and couldn't understand how I even got there in the first place. It took me a long time to figure out how to get home. I stumbled around in the very unfriendly darkness, crying and puking and practically pissing myself, for what felt like hours. Actually, it probably was hours.

I'm still not exactly sure where it all happened. I went for a walk in the daylight the next day just to see if I could remember something more, but I couldn't figure out which field it was. Grass isn't any more helpful than trees, it all looks the same.

I never thought much about how awful it was that those guys left me alone out there; all the bad things that could have happened to me drunk and on my own, out in a strange place. They didn't care about me at all. They just cared about what they wanted to do to me and when that didn't work out, I was just yesterday's garbage.

Assholes. Ass *burgers*.

I've been so scared and embarrassed and worried that they were going to tell everyone how stupid I am that I never took the time to be pissed off at how they treated me. I am now. They knew I was drunk. They *had* to. They knew I didn't really know what I was doing. They *must* have known.

Unless they were so drunk they didn't know what they were doing either, which makes everything go back around in a circle, until I'm at the beginning again and don't know what to think or do.

What does it matter, anyway? No matter what they knew or didn't know, I still went with them. I don't think they forced me. No one poured the beer down my throat.

Kal thinks I should tell so that they know they did some-thing wrong and so that they won't do it to someone else.

But who's going to get in the most trouble?

I lied to my parents, drank a shitload of alcohol under-age, and left a party with a couple of boys, who obviously thought I was interested in having a private party.

Eric and Peter drank I don't know how much alcohol underage and left a party with a really drunk girl who they took to a field out in the middle of nowhere.

They did lots wrong, but so did I. If I tell on them, I'm telling on myself. If I don't tell on them, I'm letting them get away with it, according to Kal, who isn't exactly an expert on this sort of thing. Could he be right about some of it, though? Maybe they know they did something wrong and are hop-ing no one finds out. That would mean that they might not be planning on telling anyone or showing any pictures to anyone. It really could be over.

I hate this! I don't know what's right and what's wrong.

Of course, it might not matter, seeing as I'm sitting outside in the middle of nowhere again, with no idea how I'm going to find my way home. At least this time I'm with someone I trust.

I look at Kal, who is still sleeping. I do trust him. Even though he's super weird and keeps telling me that he doesn't want friends in his life, he's actually my best friend. My BFF. I haven't told him that yet. I'm not sure he'd think it's a great thing. He used to tell me that friends were too much trouble, but I kept on telling him that everyone needs friends and that he had to let me in. Look where that got him! Lost in the woods with his head split open. And still, he's trying to help me figure my mess out.

Kal would never take a drunk girl to a field and try to screw around with her. Of course, he doesn't like to touch people. Still, I would never, ever worry that he would do something to hurt me on purpose. Even when he calls me fat, he isn't trying to be mean.

He didn't tell on me even though he was in more trouble than he's ever been in his whole life. He promised he wouldn't tell so he didn't.

I shouldn't have made him promise that. I was kind of using him.

He thinks I should tell. I should do it just to show him that I trust him and think he's smart. I owe him.

If I tell, I will be in trouble. That would be on top of the trouble I'm already in for running away. If I tell, Eric and Peter will get in trouble, and then everyone at school will probably find out that I told on them, which will make me even more unpopular than I already am.

Maybe I can be homeschooled for the rest of my life.

There are so many sounds in the dark. Rustling in the trees, footsteps breaking small branches on the ground; nocturnal animals doing their night-time things. I don't know what kinds of animals there are around here. Hopefully nothing more exciting than the deer I saw. Although, where there are deer there are often wolves or coyotes skulking around, trying to eat them. My dad taught me that most animals are afraid of humans. We're really strange to them, and they don't usually see us as dinner.

Kal doesn't seem very comfortable out here. He's pretty afraid of animals. I hope he sleeps all night. Nothing seems as scary after the sun gets up.

Speaking of getting up, it's time to wake him again. This must be the fifth time, and I know it's really bugging him, but I'm scared to stop.

"Kal! Kal!" I shake him a bit, trying to keep my voice as low as possible so as not to attract the attention of anything that might be out here.

"What?" His eyes pop open and he looks confused. He focuses on me and looks even more confused.

"Angel? Are you in my room? No one is supposed to be in my room without permission. Privacy infringement!" He's talking too loudly, and I have to shut him up.

"Kal, you're not at home. Remember? We're outside in the woods. Your head?" I'm whispering, hoping he'll get the hint.

He looks at me with very cloudy eyes, as if he has no idea who I am or what I'm talking about. He reaches up and touches his belt. He closes his eyes again and just breathes in and out slowly a few times.

"We're outside in the woods. I fell and cut my head, and you fixed it with wet wipes and my belt, which is supposed to be holding my pants. We don't know where home is, and no one has come looking for us yet. We are both missing." He's still not whispering but is at least talking a bit more quietly. He sounds sad. I can relate. This is a pretty sad situation.

"Pretty much."

"You are waking me up because you are afraid I might have a concussion."

"Right."

"Are you going to keep doing that all night?"

"Yes."

"Maybe I should just stay awake."

"I think you should try to sleep. I don't have a sore head. I'll stay awake." I don't need him noticing all the activity around us.

"All right."

"Good. Talk to you in an hour."

He doesn't answer. That could mean he's already asleep again or it could just mean that he didn't think an answer was needed. Kal isn't into small talk and doesn't need the last word in any conversation we've had. That works well because I like having the last word most of the time.

Actually most things work well with Kal and me—except for everything that's happened in the past few days. That part I'd like to forget. But other than that, he would be the world's best boyfriend, except that I'm pretty sure I gross him out on a physical level. Although, after Eric, I think maybe a boyfriend who keeps his distance would be nice.

Kal doesn't seem interested in girls. Peter the Assburger is always calling him *fag* and other words that mean gay, but I don't think he's really into guys either. I don't think he's into anyone. It's that bubble thing. I guess there's no room in there for anyone else.

I really wish there was room in there for me, at least. Then we could float off this hill or cliff or whatever it is and just keep going until we hooked up with a few crystal fairies and unicorns somewhere far away from school. What's that song? Oh, yeah, "Somewhere Over the Rainbow." That's where we'd go.

Right now, I'm pretty sure we're somewhere *under* the rainbow, where all the colors have disappeared and there isn't a good fairy anywhere to help us find our way home.

TWENTY-SIX

"What's that? What's that?" Kal sits up too fast and grabs his head in pain. His eyes look as wild as the sound that woke him up.

The howling is scarier than anything a horror movie director could dream up for a soundtrack. Loud and incredibly high pitched, screaming at us out of the darkness. Every couple of seconds there are yipping noises, like some kind of monster-sized puppy decided to join in the fun. I have images of fangs with blood dripping off them, and I have to shake my head several times to clear them away, so I can try to calm Kal down.

"It's okay. It's just wolves eating their supper. They're far away from here." At least that's how my dad always explained it to me when we were camping. It's really adult wolves attacking and killing some poor animal, most likely a

215

deer, and then ripping it to shreds while the younger wolves complain about the whole thing because they have to wait their turn.

"It's not *okay*. Stop saying that! What do you mean, eating supper? They're howling and screeching. How can they be eating? Why would it be so loud?" He's talking too fast and making terrible faces. I can't tell if they're pain faces or terror faces. I guess it doesn't make any difference. Either way, I have to help him.

"Sorry. I mean they're announcing to everyone that they've caught something to eat. They're warning other animals to stay away from their...food. It's loud so they can prove they're the boss. Just imagine a forest full of Peter Murphys, trying to sound tough."

He looks at me for a second, like he thinks I'm nuts. It's comforting to see that expression because it's the way I'm used to seeing him stare at me. It means he might be calming down.

"I've never heard Peter Murphy sound quite like that," he says, lying back down very carefully.

"Yeah, well, if I ever get a chance to kick him where the sun don't shine, Peter Assburger will be screaming louder than any wolf."

"Where the sun *doesn't* shine." Kal uses a teacher voice, but I think I saw a little bit of a smile there for a second. "Peter Assburger is a very good name. Well chosen."

"Thanks."

"What did you mean by where the sun doesn't shine? In a cave or somewhere? Would you lure him there so you can kick him?" He looks interested. I shake my head.

"No. Probably not a cave. Probably a field. The *sun don't shine* is an expression that means I want to kick him…in a sensitive place." I point in the general direction of Kal's groin. He looks confused.

"His nuts, Kal. I want to kick him in the balls. You know, the man parts."

"His scrotum." He nods and then looks like he's thinking it over. "That would certainly hurt."

"Yup. Then I'd do Eric, and I think I'd feel better about everything." Man, that would be sweet. Get them both where it hurts and then run really fast. Actually, I wouldn't have to run at all. They'd both be down and out.

"Physical violence would make you feel better?"

This is where I should do one of those social lessons he talks about. Tell him I don't condone violence, and it never solves anything.

"Definitely."

"I see. I'm not very fond of violence, even in games or on TV. It makes my stomach turn. Like the wolves howling when they kill something."

"Oh, you figured that part out."

"Yes. You're not very subtle, and I am very smart. Are you sure they're far away?" He starts to look worried again.

"Yeah. And then they won't have any interest in anything else. My dad used to tell me that hearing a kill was a good thing because it meant the local wolves were done for the night. Not that wolves like coming near us anyway." I throw on the last part quickly before he can start to panic again.

"Is it going to be morning soon?" He asks me the question and then answers it himself by looking at his watch. Diving watches light up so you can see them underwater, I guess. "Four forty-five. A couple of more hours until daylight."

"Yes. And then we can try to start moving. You need to rest. Someone will find us in the morning. I'm sure of it."

He nods slightly and closes his eyes. I don't know if he believes me or not. I don't know if *I* believe me or not.

Either way, we have to start moving again as soon as possible. I don't think anyone is going to find us lying here. As soon as it's light, I'm going up top to take a look around and really try to see if there's a way out.

I wish I had my dad's binoculars. Actually, I wish I had my dad.

My parents must be so terribly angry with me. And so scared. I never thought about that. I mean, I wanted to scare them a little bit. Twelve hours of scared, give or take. But not this much. They don't know if I'm dead or alive. My mother's probably cried so much that she's all dried out by now.

If I get out of here, I'm going to be grounded for the rest of my life. I'll be washing dishes until I'm forty and doing everyone's laundry until I'm fifty.

And it was all for nothing. I didn't change anything. I didn't fix anything. I still have to figure out what I'm supposed to tell and not tell so that I can show my face at school again.

The two hours pass more quickly than I expect. I spent most of the time whining inside my head, so I'm glad to see the sun.

"Kal? It's morning. We have to eat something and try to get moving."

"All right." His voice is muffled and sleepy.

"Are you ready to try to sit up?"

"Yes." We both work at getting him up. He sways a little once he's in a full sitting position.

"How are you feeling?" He stops moving and takes a deep breath.

"Somewhat better. I do have a dilemma though."

"Oh. A dilemma."

"A problem."

"I know what a dilemma is!" *Seriously!*

"Oh. Well, the dilemma is rather personal." He looks very uncomfortable.

"Go on." I think I know where this is going.

"I have to...urinate." The last word is whispered.

"Then we have to get you up on your feet so you can go and pee." Just in case he thinks I don't know what *urinate* means.

"There is no bathroom out here." Stating the obvious.

"No, but there are lots of trees and lucky for you, you're a guy so you can just zip and whip."

I hate peeing in the woods. I'm always afraid something is going to bite me on the ass when I crouch down. Sometimes I've tried to pull my pants down so that my butt is a bit covered but then I end up peeing on my own clothes. Guys are so lucky. They can pee anywhere, anytime.

"Zip and whip?"

"That's what my dad calls it. You're a guy. You can just

pull down your zipper and whip out your di—private part and do your business. I won't look. Promise."

His eyes look exactly the same as they did when he first heard the wolves.

"I can't do that! I've never done that."

"Then you have to hold it until we find a toilet. Which could take a while."

He sits looking at me, thinking so hard that any minute there's going to be smoke coming out of his ears.

I must be really missing my dad. I keep on using his expressions, even in my head.

"I will have to try. It is very uncomfortable, and I can't drink any more water until I empty my bladder or I will fill it even fuller and be even more uncomfortable. Can you help me to get up all the way?" His voice is very small as he says the last part. I know he really hates being touched and it's a big deal for him to ask me to help him so I don't make any stupid comments about it. I just nod and hold out my hand. He ignores it, of course, and braces himself on the rock beside him while trying to push himself to his feet. I put my hand under his elbow and try to keep him from falling back down. He's really swaying now, looking the way I felt the morning after drinking all that beer.

"Slow down. You need to give your head time to adjust here."

"All right. I'm all right. I can do this on my own now, I think." He tries a polite voice but I see his hand sneak over to his arm, and I know he really wants to rub his elbow to get the feel of me off it. A sure sign he's feeling better. It really worried me last night when he let me touch his neck.

He stands up straight, breathing slowly in and out. He tries a couple of steps and stops. I reach out, but he shakes his head slightly. He tries a couple more steps and stops again.

"I need you to walk over that way. I can't walk very far right now, not until I'm emptied out. I don't want you to listen."

"That's fine. I'm climbing the hill after you're finished anyway, so I'll just head that way now. I won't go too far until I'm sure you're all right though." I put my hands over my ears and smile at him then turn and walk toward the hill. After a few steps, I hide behind a tree so that I can watch him and make sure he doesn't fall. I know he would be about a thousand shades of embarrassed if he knew I was watching, so I really hope he doesn't notice.

I can see him standing there, staring at the tree in front of him like he's afraid it's going to bite. He looks around, just in case there's bunny rabbit watching or something. I see him struggle a bit with his fly and whatever he's got packed away in there. I turn away long enough to let him do his business and then watch again, as he slowly makes his way back to the rock. He sits back down and looks up toward where I'm standing.

I come out where he can see me, trying to look all casual, so he won't suspect I was stalking him while he urinated. That would seriously piss him off. Ha-ha. I'm so funny.

"Are you okay if I go up the hill and look around a bit?" I shout down to him.

"No, I am not okay! I am fine!" He shouts back up at me, in a strong and somewhat pissed-off voice. I hope he's just pissed at my vocabulary and didn't see me watching.

He waves at me, a little bundle of rags left behind on a rock. He seems so small and defenceless, like an abandoned fawn waiting to become wolf kibble.

I need to get moving. We have to get out of here—now.

TWENTY-SEVEN

I was awake all night, and I've eaten nothing but a granola bar in the past twenty-four hours or so, but I feel like my body is full of energy. Adrenaline most likely. That's what my dad would say.

Dad would also say that I should stop thinking about what he would say and figure things out for myself. He's a big believer in having your own mind.

He is also a big believer in me and he would tell me I can get us out of here if I set my mind to it and stop being afraid. He always tells me that the biggest enemy anyone can have is fear.

I'm not sure that's true, especially when you're lost in the woods and there are animals with big teeth that might be getting hungry. Although, it's pretty quiet here now. After all the activity last night, everyone has gone to bed for the day. I think I'm the only one making noise.

I barely finish the thought when the whole world starts to vibrate.

What now? An earthquake? The way our luck has been going, it wouldn't surprise me if Mother Nature decided to join in on the fun.

The sound is so intense that my ears start to hurt. I cover them with my hands, which dulls the pounding enough that I can recognize it.

Not an earthquake. It's a helicopter. That's a relief. An earthquake would have seriously screwed up an already completely screwed situation. I close my eyes, keeping my hands firmly against my ears, waiting for the sound to pass—for about two milliseconds, until I realize what's going on.

What the hell is wrong with me? It's a *helicopter*. Flying over *us*. Someone is looking for us! I didn't lie to Kal, after all.

I start running for the top of the hill, waving my arms and yelling. Adrenaline definitely takes over, and I can't even feel my legs. Branches slap and scratch at me, trying to slow me down, but I just smack them away and keep going.

"Here! We're here! Here!" I scream it over and over. I have to get up there before they disappear. I can still hear the sounds over my own voice. It hasn't passed over yet or maybe it's coming back. Either way, it's still here.

"Here! I'm here!" My voice is getting hoarse, but I keep yelling and running. I wish I had a big stick on fire or something dramatic like in the movies, but I don't. I just have my arms, which I keep waving over my head.

I'm finally at the top, and now I'm jumping and waving. I have to stand on the very edge of the hill, where Kal must have fallen, so that there's a chance someone can see me. It's the only place not completely covered with trees. I'm scared I'm going to end up on top of Kal, but there's no choice.

"Please see me! I'm here!" The sound is getting louder and all of a sudden I can see it. I can't believe how big it looks from here, like a huge black tank just sitting in the air. It's making a giant windstorm, and leaves are flying into my mouth and eyes. My ears are throbbing, but I'm afraid to stop flapping my arms like a demented bird, in case they don't see me.

And then suddenly there's a voice reaching out to me over the rest of the noise.

"Stay where you are. Someone will be there soon. Do not move."

The helicopter pulls up and away and after a few seconds the world is quiet again.

My head hurts, and I'm dizzy. This doesn't feel like real life. I feel like I'm dreaming, or maybe actually up on a movie screen pretending to be lost in the woods, while some hero in a helicopter talks to me from the sky.

If—when—we make it out of here, I'm definitely taking Kal to the movies. My treat.

Kal. Shit! He's still waiting on me. Did he hear? I want to go down and check on him; make sure he knows we're going to be rescued, but I'm afraid to move in case someone comes back and can't find us.

I have to tell him without moving away from here. He probably heard everything, but I need to make sure. I don't want him worrying any longer than he has to.

"Kal! Did you hear?" I shout it down the hill. I can barely see him from here, but I hope he can hear me. I think he answers, but I'm not sure.

"Kal! I'm staying here. We're safe now! Just wait!" I scream it as loudly as my voice can manage, and then collapse onto the grass. Sitting down, I hug my knees and rest my head on them, closing my eyes for the first time in what feels like forever.

It's over. Someone is coming to take us home.

My throat hurts from all of the yelling, and my eyes are stinging from all of the leaves and dirt that the flying tank threw into them.

I feel like I'm going to cry. I look down and notice that my knees are damp. I guess I'm already crying. I sob and hiccup. Snot pours down my face and onto my pants, making a gross mess. I can't seem to stop, everything and everyone that's been crammed up inside of me making my life hell is turning into liquid and pouring out of my body. If I don't stop I'm going to float away, and they'll never find me.

I cry and cry until I run out of fluids. I'm so tired now. I just want to sleep, but I know I can't. I have to keep watch and make sure they find me when they come back again. I'll just sit for a minute and then get up so they can see me better.

We're going home. It's only been a few days, but it feels like forever since I've seen my parents. I don't know what they're going to do when they see me. I don't think it's going to be pretty.

If it wasn't for Kal, I think I might just keep on going and try to find a nice tree to live in.

I close my eyes for a second, just to rest them a bit before the next episode of my screwed up life starts.

My Screwed Up Life. Now that's a movie I could star in.

"Angel? Is that your name?" The voice pushes into me and I open my eyes. A woman is leaning over me with her hand on my shoulder. I blink my eyes, trying to focus, but her face is as blurry as my brain. This can't be the helicopter person already. It's only been a couple of minutes.

"Yes. That's me." My voice sounds shaky.

"Sorry to wake you, but I think it's time for you to come home," she says kindly, with a small smile.

Wake me? I was actually asleep? Great. The one thing I had to do was stay awake for a few more minutes so I could make sure they found Kal, and instead, I take a nap.

"Kal! He's down there!" I'm yelling at her as I start to struggle to my feet.

"Kal? There's a third person?" She looks startled and jumps up, looking down the hill.

"No. Just me and Kal." Third person? What is she talking about? We have to get to Kal!

"We found Frederick. He told us you've been taking care of him. They're fixing him up now and taking him to the hospital. We're taking you there, too. Who is Kal?"

"Oh, right. Sorry. Just a nickname. Frederick. Right. That's who I meant. Just me and Frederick. I don't need a hospital. He hit his head. but I'm okay." I think I'm still yelling but I seem to have lost my volume control.

"You've been missing for several days. We need to have you checked over. Your parents are meeting us there." She's using a very quiet, calm voice, the kind cops use on TV when they're trying to negotiate with some guy holding a knife. She obviously thinks I'm nuts.

"They are going to seriously kill me." Maybe I should take her with me to negotiate with my parents.

She laughs a little and puts her arm around my shoulder to help me walk. Good thing, too, because I think I might fall down if she lets go.

"They are going to seriously be glad to see you. Then they might want to kill you."

Now I laugh a little—a very little because my face is tired.

We walk down the side of the hill that Kal and I walked up. There are all kinds of people at the bottom of the hill. I don't know any of them.

We walk back through the woods for a bit and it feels like we're going back the same way Kal and I walked yesterday.

Yesterday. Was it only one day?

It takes only a few minutes for us to come out into a clearing where there is an ambulance waiting. Which means there is a road nearby. We were this close? How could we have missed it?

"Just a bit farther, and you can lie down for the rest of the trip."

"I don't need an ambulance. Kal does. Where is he?"

"He's fine. He was taken out a different way."

A different way. We spent the whole night in the woods and she's telling me there were *two* different exit routes this close to where we were?

"Shit!" I slap my hand over my mouth. I didn't mean to say that out loud. But seriously, this is so stupid.

"It's all right. We'll take good care of him."

"No, it's not that. We walked right by the way out. Probably about ten times. How could I be so stupid?"

"If you don't know the area, it's hard to navigate. The trees are thick here and you can be five minutes from a road and have no idea. People get lost out this way fairly often."

"Really?" It felt like we were the only ones in the history of everything.

"Really. The important thing is that you kept yourself and your friend safe. You did a good job fixing up his head. Doesn't sound stupid to me. Now, get some rest. These guys are going to take care of you." She gives my arm a squeeze and walks off. Two ambulance guys help me into the back, where I lie down on a stretcher. I feel a bit silly in the back of an ambulance when I'm not actually hurt, but I'm too tired to think about it for very long.

My eyes shut seconds after the doors do, and I don't open them again until I hear my mother's voice.

twenty-eight

"Frederick. You have a guest. Do you want to see her?"

"All right."

"Aren't you going to ask me who it is?" My mother is standing in the doorway of my room looking at me. I have to keep my door open these days, as she seems to need to look at me a lot.

"I only know one girl. I can make an educated guess."

My mother smiles a little and shakes her head slightly. She doesn't look very happy that I have a visitor. I suspect that she doesn't really want me to be friends with Angel anymore. She hasn't actually said that to me, but she has lots of suggestions about how I could find other people to spend time with at school.

Not that I've been back to school yet. My record is destroyed forever. My teachers have been e-mailing my homework assignments, so I haven't technically fallen behind in any of my classes. It's rather a peaceful way to go to school. Maybe all school should be done this way. No teachers interrupting my reading. No Despisers interrupting my lunch. No friends interrupting my life.

My head doesn't hurt much now. The doctor at the hospital said I had a concussion, which means I had a traumatic injury to my head. Brains have the consistency of gelatin, and they're usually protected by cerebrospinal fluid, so you aren't hurt by normal little bumps and bruises. But if you hit your head hard enough, your brain actually slides around and bounces off your skull, which is a very disturbing thing to think about. Everything got jostled around in there and I've had to stay home all week so that my mother can stare at me all day and make sure that the symptoms aren't getting worse. Concussions usually produce temporary symptoms, like pain and confusion, but sometimes they can result in bleeding in the brain. I don't want my brain to bleed on my inside. I did enough bleeding on my outside.

My colors are so jumbled up that the inside of my mind is the color of mud, which isn't surprising, seeing as I spent almost twenty-four hours lying in the dirt. At least mud is better than blood.

If I said that out loud, Angel would think I was making a joke and punch me in the arm.

Just as I think her name, I look up and see her in the doorway. She's just standing there staring at me like my mother does.

"Hi," I say to her, starting the conversation for a change.

Maybe the concussion has altered my social skills.

"Hi. I hope I didn't wake you up. You had your eyes closed."

"Oh. No, I was just thinking." I didn't even realize that my eyes were closed. I have to check and see if that's another symptom.

"How are you feeling?"

"It doesn't hurt as much now. I feel tired a lot, but my mother says that is to be expected as I had a trauma."

"A trauma caused by me. Your mother must totally hate me." Angel comes in uninvited and sits on my desk chair beside the bed. Her eyes seem sad to me, but I can't be sure. She might just be tired, like I am.

"I don't think my mother hates you. The doctor told her that you did a good job looking after me, so she is grateful to you. She isn't too happy that you got me involved in your problems though. I think she's glad I made a friend but wishes I had picked someone else." I close my eyes again. That was a lot of words, and my brain is very tired from all the bouncing.

"I can't blame her for that. Do you hate me?"

The question opens my eyes again. "No. Why would I hate you?"

"Oh, I don't know. I lied to you, then I made you lie for me and go to Castleford on a scary bus for me and get lost in the woods for me—just for starters."

I'm not sure that she *made* me do anything. I have free will. I think. "I don't hate you. I don't think I hate anyone."

"Oh. Well, that's good. I guess." She smiles a little but

her eyes still look sad. "Robert told me that the kids at school are spreading rumors about you and me. They are saying that we were…that we are…um…together. A couple. That we… did things."

Peter Murphy might have to come up with some new ways of insulting me if he thinks I'm in love with Angel instead of Robert.

"I guess you can tell them the truth when you get back to school." She shrugs her shoulders.

"I'm not telling anyone anything." I shrug my shoulders too. I was going to shake my head, but I'm still afraid to do that in case it makes my brain worse.

"Did you swear another oath?" She smiles at me again but this time it creeps up into her eyes, and she looks like herself. It makes me want to smile back. So I do.

"Don't tell, don't tell, don't tell." The oath that started it all.

"I won't tell if you don't," she says, wiggling her eyebrows up and down, as if she said something funny.

"What?"

"Nothing, Kal. Just an expression."

"I don't like most expressions. They are often hard to understand."

"Yeah, well, sometimes life is hard to understand. My mom wants me to go to the police."

"I went to the police." I wonder if she'll meet Officer Dummkopf.

"I know."

"It's not so hard. Just answer the questions and don't try

to become invisible." That part didn't work at all. Angel looks at me and smiles a little.

"Okay. I'll try not to. I'm not so worried about it being hard. I just didn't think this was the kind of thing you talk to the police about, but Mom said it isn't up to me to decide that."

"Moms are often right." My mom is going to think she's right for the rest of my life. I don't know how I'm going to get her to stop staring at me. Maybe she's afraid I am going to become invisible and disappear again.

"They always think they are, anyway."

"I agree. So are you going to go to the police?"

"I guess so. I can't exactly tell my mother no these days."

"Do you think Eric and Peter will go to jail?"

"I asked my mom the same question. She said she doesn't think so but they need to talk to the police so they understand how serious this was. How they should know that it's wrong to take someone to a field all alone and do things to her when she's out of it. My dad said that leaving me there defenceless was just as bad or worse, and that the he'd be happy to talk to the guys instead of letting the cops do it. I think they're safer with the cops, personally. Anyway, my mother said that it's up to the police to decide what to do, not me. My job is to tell them what happened. And to stay away from booze for the rest of my life."

"Do you find it odd that people say 'the police,' as if you are seeing all of them, or as if there is only one of them?"

She looks at me as if she finds *me* odd. "Sure. I find lots of things odd."

"Like me."

She laughs. "Ha. You made a joke! But seriously, Kal. You are one of the oddest people I know. And one of the nicest."

"I find you to be rather odd, also. You're thinner than you used to be."

"Thanks."

"It wasn't a compliment. Just an observation."

"Of course. I wasn't thinking. Anyway, I guess I have to go ruin my life again now."

"Going to the police will ruin your life?"

"Maybe. It'll make school hell, anyway. No matter what happens to the guys, no one at school will ever talk to me again."

"I will."

"That's good. Maybe one friend is enough." She looks at me for another second and then walks away.

When my brain is functioning better, I'm going to have to think about everything that happened. I'm going to have to try to figure out how I ended up at a police station and on a bus and lost in the woods all because of a girl who talks too much and punches me on the arm when she thinks I'm being funny. A girl who thinks I'm cool and calls me her friend. A girl who tells me things that I'm not supposed to tell anyone else.

I think I should tell Angel how I feel about movie theaters. I'm pretty sure she would understand.

I wonder if she still wants to go to a movie with me some day? I think that's something I could actually like to do.

I'll just have to remember to tell her to keep her hands off my popcorn.

"Angel? Are you all right?"

I look at her and she smiles at me.

Kal was right, the police aren't so scary—as long as you don't try to become invisible.

"Yeah, sorry. I was just...thinking."

"Are you sure you're all right to do this today?"

"Yes. I'm sure. Let's just do it."

"Okay then, I'd like you to tell me about the Friday night, a week before you ran away."

Kal's big, serious eyes dance into my mind and stare at me. I take a deep breath.

And then I start to tell.

acknowledgments

I want to express my deepest thanks to my editor Carolyn Jackson, who has been my literary champion from the very beginning and continues to support my writing with patience and understanding while always managing to find even the tiniest of mistakes so that I can create my best manuscript. I also want to share my heartfelt appreciation for Margie Wolfe, Kathryn Cole, and all of the wonderful staff at Second Story Press for their continued faith in me and their hard work in presenting my stories to the world.

As always, thanks to my husband David, who listens to every word of every manuscript revision and even manages to stay awake…most of the time.

And finally, to my nephew Braydon and the legion of my former students living under the ever expanding umbrella that is ASD—you all make the world a more interesting and valuable place by your very presence. The rest of us have a great deal to learn from you should we ever be lucky enough to see the world through your eyes.

about the author

LIANE SHAW was an educator for more than 20 years, both in the classroom and as a special education resource teacher. She is the author of *Time Out*, *The Color of Silence*, *Fostergirls*, and *thinandbeautiful.com*. Now retired from teaching, Liane lives with her family in the Ottawa Valley. Liane likes to hear from her fans, so contact her at lianeshaw2014@outlook.com and check out her website: lianeshaw.com.